360 Eagle Nest Ln SW
Rochester, MN 55902

The 5th World

THOMAS COOHILL

The 5th World

On December 21, 2012 the 4th Mayan World ends...

Cuchulain Press
Loudonville, New York
2007

For

Patricia

Joseph

Thomas

& Matthew

Copyright 2007 Thomas Coohill
5thWorld@coohill.com

All rights reserved. Printed in the United States of America. No part of this book may be used or reproduced in any manner whatsoever without written permission except in the case of brief quotations embodied in critical articles or reviews.

Cover Art by Barbara Fugate
www.barbarafugate.com

*In Huehuetenango, in the highlands of Guatemala,
the Mayans carve 26 masks of the devil, all in red;
each represents an evil: the corrupt politician,
the wicked lawyer, the wayward priest.
Then they carve one in green. He is the most evil,
the devil you don't know.*

1

Maria was in a corn field, the tassels honey-colored by the waning sun. She looked around - field on two sides, temples in front and, at her side, the beautiful woman she had just met. The woman glided forward and beckoned. Maria knew to follow. They walked together silently through the field, the corn leaves slapping Maria's arms, the mist rising like sighs from the underworld, then they came to the square and entered the magnificent complex of Tikal. The woman motioned to Maria to follow her up the 52 stairs of Temple II and onto the platform. Behind the altar stood a Mayan priest; sloping forehead, scythe-shaped nose, receding chin. His feathered headdress billowed in the warm breeze; his arms raised in prayer; he bowed his head. They stood at the edge and looked down 80 feet to the stone plaza below.

The woman spoke. "I will show you how to fly."

Before Maria could respond, the woman jumped from the platform, fell 20 feet, then rose in a wide arc up and over the startled Maria. She watched as the woman circled in the air, sometimes above the temples, sometimes over the fields. The woman's graceful moves controlled her flight. It looked so effortless. The woman flew back to the platform and hovered like a hummingbird. "Come, join me," she said.

Maria looked blank.

"It is easy," said the woman. "Just jump and you will fly."

Maria shook her head.

"What I tell you is true," said the woman. "But the commitment is yours alone."

"I can't fly," said Maria.

"You must believe."

"No, I don't want to die."

"Belief is enough," said the woman so serene, so confident.

"Will you catch me if I fall?" said Maria.

"That is not belief."

Maria wanted to fly, more than anything. She wanted to be like this woman calm, assured, in control. She inched toward the edge of the platform. The woman smiled.

"I can't push off," said Maria.

Then the woman changed. Wings sprouted from her back, the tips came forward, and beckoned Maria like the fingers of a welcoming hand.

Maria teetered at the edge.

The angel moved back and down, her face glowing. She nodded.

Maria shuddered, closed her eyes and stepped off the platform.

She fell, screaming, but then something inside her made her stop. She willed herself to be calm, to think of herself flying.

Halfway to the ground, her descent slowed. She was near the middle of the stairway, at eye level with a glowing image of The Virgin of Guadalupe. Maria looked at the haunting, humble, olive face, framed in shades of blue and red. The figure of the Mother, radiating in transparent beauty, sun at her back, horned moon at her feet, held up by a babe. Angels attended her and, above, the Holy Spirit spread His wings. After a few seconds Maria realized that the image was stationary. She had stopped falling.

Maria turned in the air, saw the angel, and rose to meet her.

"Follow me," said the angel.

First they flew down along the plaza, then raced up parallel to the stairs; above the altar; above the outstretched arms of the priest. The angel flew back and to the side. Maria followed. Now they soared above the complex, and looked down on the hollowed site, the twin temple towers rising to the heavens, the splendor of the architecture.

They flew higher: up above the vast place of worship, the view like the aerial postcard Maria had sent home last summer.

"We can go farther," the angel said.

Maria sat up in bed, the dream so vivid her pupils were constricted as if in bright light. As they dilated, Maria realized where she was. She wanted to be elsewhere.

She lay back, turned on her side, and tried to reenter her dream.

2

There are Worlds and Worlds within Worlds

Saturday, December 15, 2012
3 days after the Feast of
Our Lady of Guadalupe
5:30 AM

It was no use. The elation from the dream kept Maria awake. Although she was tired, she got out of bed, went to the bathroom, and looked in the mirror. Gone was the face she had known: smooth olive skin, fine featured, lit by youth and the wonder of life. In its place was another, stronger but curiously less attractive: a long brow centered over a thin nose, wide black eyes, full lips (almost too full), strong chin. None of the parts one would pick but beautiful taken together. Another source of the envy people felt towards her. Or perhaps it was her willfulness, pride in her accomplishments, selfishness. She could wiggle her ears, arch both brows at once, whistle like a man (her mother said, "When a girl whistles the Blessed Mother cries").

Maria was 5'8", 126 pounds, size 8 shoe, had long thin fingers, a tight ass (but not a boy's ass), nice breasts (not too large), sensuous (when she let herself go, put-offish otherwise), unforgiving of even little faults (except in those she needed for her work), apolitical except when woman's lib suited her (scornful of it otherwise), confident, and hard to rattle. She made sure she didn't laugh too much (a sign of weakness), and never giggled, even as a child. She had a weakness for men who ignored her, her robotic dog, Aquafina, and mirrors. She was hard on underachievers, lazy people, smokers (she thought second-hand smoke extended for miles), and men who kow-towed to women (even her). She ran fingers through her auburn hair, framing her face with the layered ends, and turned to check her torso, full front and in profile.

"Not bad," she decided, wondering if it was the workouts or genetics. She pulled up her designer jeans, stretched, yawned, and filled the basin with warm water.

The dream had a calming effect on her. The sensation of flying filled her with peace. She wished she could call up a dream when ever she wanted it, like a video.

Maria had a bachelor's in computer science from Carnegie-Mellon, a master's in electrical engineering from Georgia Tech, and a Ph. D. in Computer Systems and Remote Sensing from Caltech. She accepted a position in Pittsburgh with some disappointment. She didn't want to be that close to her parents, but Infinity offered her up-to-the-minute facilities, a large research budget, and freedom to pursue her interests. These involved the design of a large-scale networking system to interface the Worldwide Web. They were lucky to get her. Maria had few peers, and she knew it.

She washed off the remaining soap, rinsed twice with water, then raised her face, hands on either cheek, and looked in the mirror again. Next to her face was another.

Maria shrieked. "Who are you?"

"A friend."

Maria stepped to the side, picked up a pair of scissors, and turned to face the woman.

"How did you get in here?"

"I have come to help you - and your kind."

With her other hand, Maria reached for a can of hair spray and pointed the nozzle at the woman.

"Get out right now, before I call the cops."

The woman backed away and sat on the rim of the tub. "Maria, do not be afraid."

It was the angel from the dream.

Maria started shaking, her breath rapid. She felt dizzy, faint, unable to hold the can or the scissors - her only defenses. And then, almost imperceptibly, her breathing slowed, and a gentle calm washed over and through her. It emanated from the angel sitting in her bathroom, so poised, so calm, so accepting.

"I've seen you before," said Maria.

"Yes. I came to you last night."

Maria put down the can and rubbed her eyes. "I need a minute."

"Take your time, Maria. I will wait."

Maria put the scissors down, placed her hands on the sink, and leaned backwards, catching her breath.

Neither spoke for several minutes.

Then Maria said, "I don't believe this. I'm hallucinating or still dreaming."

The angel waited.

"You can't be real," said Maria. "You'll go away in a minute."

The angel sat there, still, hands crossed on her lap, looking, not staring, at Maria.

"I mean, this can't be. There are no angels, not really."

The angel smiled again.

"Now, you just tell me who you are and how you got in here."

"Maria," said the angel, "I am real, as real as you are. We existed before the first human. Your doors and walls are no obstacles to us. We can come and go as we wish."

Maria shook her head to break the spell and said, "Look, I don't want any part of you. Get out of here."

"But Maria, I have always been with you," said the angel. "Only now have I chosen to manifest myself."

"Sure, you're my guardian angel. Right?"

"Correct, Maria. You saw me when you were a child, but you have forgotten all about those times."

"Look, I'm not even Catholic anymore. I've given up that mumbo-jumbo."

"Maria, look at you. You think you have all the answers. You think you are so smart. But you do not even know who or what you are. You do not realize that deep down you are lost and confused. And you do not know why. No matter how hard you work, or how well you do, you are not satisfied. You feel hollow inside. I have come to lead you back to the path."

Another thing Maria noted that was odd about the woman was her voice. It was enchanting, clear, and resonant, soft yet penetrating, not made by flesh and blood vocal cords, but pure, like a perfect instrument played by a heavenly hand.

"I'm just where I want to be. I have a good job, great apartment, the respect of my colleagues," Maria said.

"You need much more."

"How dare you presume to talk to me like this? I don't know you - I don't want to know you. I have a busy schedule today. I don't have time for you. If you're my guardian angel you would have known that."

"Show me the palm of your left hand," said the angel.

"Why? If you were a real angel you would know what's there."

"The Mark of the Turning."

"What?" said Maria, bringing the palm to her face.

"That was placed there as a sign," said the angel.

Maria looked again at the brown pigment that stained the intersection of her life lines, forming a small cigar-shaped rod. The dermatologist said it was stimulated pigmentation, but his attempt to remove it by laser had failed. Maria folded her hand again.

"What does it mean?" she asked.

"It is a sign. The rod is the Mayan symbol for 5. The turning is the Fifth World."

"Please, not me. Not now. Perhaps we can discuss this after the holidays."

"We have no time to wait Maria, we need you now."

"So do my parents. Christmas is just 10 days away and I have to be with them."

"YOU HAVE BEEN CHOSEN!"

"Oh, God, don't tell me I'm pregnant."

"Far more, Maria. You are the woman who will save the world."

Maria left her apartment in a daze and started across the parking lot to her car. Her adrenaline was pumping, keeping her at the edge of collapse. She was concentrating on what the angel had told her. It was unbelievable. Maybe the vision would go away. Maybe she was still dreaming. There must be a rational explanation.

She turned the key in the ignition. The radio kicked in. "Angels we have heard on high, sweetly singing o'er the plains." She punched the off button. How could she absorb it all? Should she? If it were true, what would happen next? And how should she begin the task the angel had given her? And why did Ariel, as the angel called herself, insist she start immediately and yet still finish what she had already planned for the day?

"Other people are involved in this," Ariel had said. "I will tell you when to act."

"But what else will I be doing?" Maria had asked.

"Your skills, which the Lord has given you, are needed. You will design a new machine for our use. It will use the Excalibur processor to integrate the World Wide Web for our purpose. Through you we will control the message."

"What message?"

"All in time."

When the angel left, Maria called Elaine. "Are you sure you don't mind my coming over?"

"Of course not," replied Elaine.

"Well, it's almost Christmas."

"Oh?"

"See you in 20 minutes."

It irked Maria to interrupt her plans, disturbing her sense of pace and order. She felt controlled, something she thought she had left behind in college. "My God," she thought. "Get a grip."

She was aiming the car instead of driving it.

"Elaine, this place is a mess," said Maria, looking past the jumble and the dirt.

"Looks fine to me," Elaine said.

Maria held her breath, then summoned the strength to enter the fetid apartment that Elaine called home. She knew her nose would adapt to the smell, her eyes to the clutter, her brain to the confusion.

"I told you that dust and mold are the enemy of electronics," she said.

Elaine swept the five day old, half-eaten, mold-covered sandwich, still in the plastic deli box, off the table with her left hand. It fell into the waste paper basket below, little puffs of spores rising above the lid.

"Satisfied?"

"I was hoping you'd changed," said Maria.

"And I was hoping you'd stop being my thesis adviser."

Elaine Masters' life was a loss by most standards. Short and chubby, her pear shape was perfect for sitting in a chair; grey teeth rotting in her mouth; mouse brown hair matted into stringy knots. She might have been attractive once, but it was difficult to tell now that she indulged her whims so. She planted herself back in the chair facing the computer, and waited for Maria to acclimate.

Maria started again. "Elaine, I have good work for you if you're available."

"How good?"

"The Excalibur."

Maria didn't mention pay, since Elaine rarely showed interest in money. Maria would simply give her cash once in a while, as she needed it.

"How can you get your hands on an Excalibur? I thought they weren't finished yet."

"There's no need for long explanations. I have perfect contacts. This is high-level stuff. You just have to know that I can get it here by tomorrow. The project has to be ready for testing by Wednesday."

"You really set deadlines. Wednesday? Why so soon?"

"It has to be installed Friday, the 21st," said Maria.

"Why?"

"Elaine, this is a complicated project - no one else can pull it off but us. Maybe not even us. I don't even know all the details yet. Without you, the whole scheme fails."

Elaine pulled on her lower lip, chewed the knuckle on her thumb, then moved to the nail. She knew how Maria was, always big projects that somehow got done, pushing as if it were the end of the world, yet stingy with her compliments when the job was completed. And now she was claiming that this was bigger, secret, in a God-awful rush. "Why does Maria have to keep me in the dark? Why doesn't she trust me?" Elaine wondered. She reached for a Little Debby bar.

Sure, Elaine knew Maria was a genius, in a way. Sure, no one but Elaine really liked her. Sure, Maria would take all the credit. But when you worked with her you were working on the stuff of dreams. And there was the matter of Elaine's landlord, demanding the back rent, threatening to throw her out. She needed something to tide her over. The thought of moving her stuff, so perfectly arranged to her purpose, was unthinkable.

"Clue me in some more," said Elaine.

"Okay, but this is top secret, beyond any government level," said Maria, as she sketched out the minimum information needed to convince Elaine from the little Ariel had told her.

There really was never any doubt. When Maria asked, Elaine delivered.

"Okay, I'm on line," she said.

Maria pulled up the other chair in the room, cleaned off an area on the desktop, and started drawing her plans.

"The Excalibur is said to incorporate prismatic twisting," Maria began, explaining how that would give a 3-D effect. Then she guessed it would have thrust-drivers to download images at a rate of 60 screens per second, four times as fast as the human eye.

"That will allow us to project video beyond any quality out there now," she said.

But it was the raw power of the chip that made it so essential.

"Even if the rumors are only half-true, it can handle a program of 8 peta-bytes. That's where WONK comes in."

Maria sketched out the high points of Worldwide Online Network Kingdom, the program she would write. WONK had the unique ability to override video terminal on/off switches and bypass filters, like the V-chip, and transmit a live signal to the screen of any TV or computer.

"Wasn't this part of your thesis?" Elaine asked.

"Yes, but we never tried to get it funded. Too expensive, the chips weren't powerful enough, and besides, its purpose is illegal."

Elaine never blinked. "Illegal" meant nothing to her, especially coming from Maria.

"But all this is useless unless Excalibur can be wired at a no-fault level," Maria continued.

She explained what that would take. First, Maria had to scope the architecture, then, if all those details were correct, Elaine would need to figure out how to place the chip in a parallel matrix circuit so it could perform as promised. One bad connection, one faulty transistor, one negative feedback loop, and the system would destruct.

"Can you do it?" asked Maria.

"Sure."

Maria laughed. Elaine was the most positive person she knew. Ask her to design a circuit that would work on the surface of the Sun and she'd say, "Sure." And Maria needed the skills that went with that optimism. If the two of them couldn't do it, no one could. That was why they had been chosen.

It took six hours for Maria and Elaine to decide how the chips should be wired, how to install the program, the size of the box, the redundancy, the small fan and metal dissipaters to prevent overheating. Elaine worked at the design, Maria the numbers. They sat and put it all together.

Interfacing with NextNet would be no problem; feeding that signal into a regular TV would be difficult but manageable; building the search engines to turn on remote terminals may be almost impossible, except that Maria could program asynchronous transfer pulses into her system. In order to pipeline all this they would need a powerful workstation, but the Excalibur should be able to do it; the new Smart View would give them the high video and voice resolution they needed, and multi-channel signaling would give them the access.

All that assumed Maria's program would work on such a large scale.

"You have no time constraints?" said Maria.

"No. I'll order in. I've lived on pizza for more than a week. When you come back please bring me some *RedBull*, lots of pretzels, a couple of boxes of Mallomars, some Twinkies, peanut butter and crackers, Eskimo Pies, maybe some cheese."

"You won't live to be thirty."

"Who wants to?" said Elaine.

"Maybe you will if this works."

"What's the difference? My heaven is full of computers."

"You may get your heaven right here on earth."

Maria stepped through the narrow aisle that separated the two piles of Elaine's junk and walked to the door. She held it open.

"Thank you, Elaine."

"No problema, Bwana. What's this project called?"

Maria thought for a moment, then said, "Savior."

3

Saturday
3:00 PM

Maria Mercedes Montez, M³ to her closest friends, was named after the Virgin of Guadalupe , just like her mother, Rosa. Rosa, born on the sacred day December 12th, was named Rosemary after both the Virgin and the Castilian roses that bloomed in the dead of winter and out of place on the hill of Tepeyac, north of Mexico City, where the Virgin appeared to Juan Diego Cuauhtlatoatzin in 1531. After her daughter was born, Rosa dropped the Mary from her name. And, since they were from Guatemala, the Montezes believed that the Virgin was the manifestation of the indigenous goddess Tonantzin. Catholic/Mayan churches in the Mayan areas even threw pine needles on the church floors to remind them of the jungle origins of their old gods.

This link to the poor was forged by this apparition who embodied the perspective of Matthew 11:25 that truth would be "hid… from the wise…but revealed…unto babes."

Then there was Salvador. Maria's father was named after the Black Christ of Esquipulas, the second-most revered icon in Latin America. And he claimed that Montez was for the mountain on which the Virgin talked to the peasant Juan. Maria even called their only dog "Saint," since Sal had brought him home on All Saints' Day. She was far from believing any of this now.

The next few hours weren't going to be pleasant. First, Rosa's birthday party had been delayed three days because Maria couldn't come on the 12th, the Virgin's Feast day. Then Maria, always reluctant, agreed to have dinner with her parents but couldn't come until three. She tried to be out of town for these parties since her parents insisted on inviting her estranged husband whom, in their minds, she was still married to. It was one of only a few concessions Maria gave to Rosa and Sal; that is, she hadn't divorced John yet. Maria was circumspect about family things and knew the divorce would happen someday. She wasn't interested in meeting anyone else anyway, so why stir things up? Rosa was so pitiful when Maria first brought it up, crossing herself dozens of times and weeping. Maria let it pass. Besides, John was more likely to find someone soon and then insist on a divorce. That would lower him in their eyes and they could get it finished. But these get-togethers added strain. She never liked family gatherings anyway, same old, same old. And now they insist on inviting her ex. Only good thing about going was that she wouldn't be nagged by the "Honor thy mother and father" thing.

But how could she focus on them when her mind was on the Excalibur? The thought of having the super-chip in her hands thrilled her. Everyone wanted to see if it lived up to even half of its hype. And how would Ariel get her one?

The small two-story house in the Point Breeze section of Pittsburgh was rimmed with lights. On the roof were angels, attending the manger of the Christ Child; three Wise Men knelt just above the gutters, offering gifts. Maria parked in front and entered by the kitchen door. Rosa was at the stove, stirring something. Sure - the very Guatemalan diet that made them so much shorter than Maria.

Maria noticed that her parents had failed to listen to her again. Her father's consumption was no better; the hacking cough more frequent now, and little spots of blood covered his handkerchief. He had been diagnosed with TB years ago when night sweats kept him awake even on the coolest evenings. Now he was beginning to lose weight, the sign of final stages.

By comparison, Rosa was healthier but still had little energy, watched too much TV, overate, and refused all of Maria's efforts to reform her. How could she let herself go so much? Had she no pride? Maria was embarrassed to meet them in the presence of friends. They looked so old.

"Listen," she said. "Your membership in the health club is up for renewal. Should I bother?" No answer.

Maria put her gifts down near the fireplace and took off her coat.

"How's my little girl?" asked Sal Montez.

"Fine, Dad. It smells good in here."

And so began the ritual of visiting. Maria asked about their health, her parents lobbed inane questions about her job and her happiness. It served as small talk. The west corner of the living room was dominated by a large spruce, a silver star with an angel on top. Several angel bells hung from the limbs. Maria hadn't noticed them before.

"Hummph! I bought those years ago when Kaufmann's was still open," said Rosa.

Ornaments from Maria's childhood stood out: a little Guatemalan Chicken Bus with her name over the window, a pink mouse inside a transparent ball, a doll dressed as Santa Claus. There were three unopened presents under the tree. Maria added two more, as her eyes scanned the familiar surroundings.

"Are you all right?" asked Sal.

"I'm fine, fine. Too much coffee, I guess."

"John will be here in a minute," called Rosa from the kitchen.

"Mama, don't," said Maria.

"You'll live through it. It makes your mother happy," said Sal. "Besides, John is good company."

Maria hadn't seen John in a year. Their separation was proceeding and they had asked the Church for an annulment, more for her parents' sake than anything else. Rumor had it that the Church was getting more liberal on these things, something from Corinthians about having to fulfill the six points for a sacramental marriage. Fail three of these and you got your ticket out. Typical new-age dodge.

The front doorbell rang.

To Maria, John seemed handsomer than before. Maybe she was just horny. He was better dressed too, probably since his paintings were beginning to sell. She noticed he was putting on weight.

He greeted Maria. How she hated his charm. It was aggravating.

Her sharp reply hung in the air until Sal said, "Wait 'til you see what Rosa got me for Christmas."

The formality of opening the early presents began, especially important this year since both Maria and John couldn't make it for Christmas Eve. Maria had bought her parents matching electronic personal organizers - just the thing for a retired couple with little to do - and for Rosa's birthday, a gift certificate for a 62" DLP TV so Sal could watch the Steelers in style. She'd get a techie at work to install it for them.

"Everyone's watching them, Mom and Dad. You might as well get in the swing of things. Just play with the remote for a few weeks and you'll be fine."

She added the new Catholic Latin channel for Rosa. For Sal it was the NFL Prime-Time package.

Naturally, her parents gave her housewife things - the latest cookbook and a Martha Stewart video. They gave John a copy of Durer's Apocalypse engravings, which pleased him since his paintings dealt with the same theme.

"That Apocalypse scares me," said Rosa.

"We Lutherans call it The Revelation," said John. "And it's supposed to be an uplifting message written in a secret code that only the faithful can decipher."

"Why would God do that?"

"Well, He works in strange ways, I guess."

John gave Rosa a subscription to *People*.

"Just the thing!" she cried.

He gave Sal a 1/4-inch portable drill.

The last gift focused everyone's attention. Maria didn't want to accept it, but she had no choice. She looked at the "To: Maria, From: John" label and reluctantly opened the wrapping, saying, "But, John, I had no time to shop..."

"Neither did I," he replied.

The present was one of his recent drawings for The War of the Angels, from a series for *Paradise Lost*.

After receiving the engraving, Maria said, "Wow, this is great. How can you tell which are the good angels and which are the bad?"

"No problem," said John. "The bad ones are more magnificent."

"That scares me, too," said Rosa.

In a space beyond this realm, two beings met.

"Ave! O Frater nefastus!" said the first. [Hail! O abominable brother.]

At first they talked of the times before the Fall, when they were brothers, praising the Lord. Then they spoke of the present.

"The battle is joined," said the first.

"And we are ready," said the other.

"Know that I will destroy you."

"Your kind's power is weakening. When will you learn that threats cannot frighten the learned?"

"The human will hearken to me."

"Never. Her soul aches for release."

"What will you tempt her with?" said the first.

"And what will you use to scare her?"

"Your envy of them is your doom."

"He placed it in our hearts. Why were they created, and why like Him?"

"It was not ours to question. He created us for a purpose, too," said the first.

"What? To be messengers to them?"

"To love and serve Him without question."

"But they question, don't they?" said the other.

"They are made from matter, whose forms let them learn from their mistakes. They forgive themselves and others."

"Like Him!"

"Our power is great and cannot change. When God wanted to save the world, did He become one of us? No, He became one of them," said the first.

"I will not stoop to please Him."

"He knows. Your kind will never return."

"But we know man and we will draw him away."

The first angel slipped a hand inside its robe, grasped its sword, and withdrew it with a flourish. "We have fought this battle before."

"And we shall again. Our determination is endless," said the other.

Then they parted.

Rosa asked about John's family, running through the list of brothers and sisters. Maria didn't listen. Sal started a story about Maria as a teenager, more embarrassing than interesting. When he finished, he turned on the TV. John sat down to watch, and Maria went to the kitchen.

Twenty minutes later Rosa, who insisted on cooking even for her birthday, announced, "Dinner is ready," and they moved to the dining area. Sal stood over the ham and began to slice it.

"Thinner," said Rosa.

After everything was passed, Sal raised his wine glass, "To happier times."

Each time Rosa turned the conversation toward them, John or Maria turned it back to something else. For the first time, Maria thought of it as a game, more enjoyable than painful. Her parents never stopped eating to talk; it all went together. They ate for over an hour.

Back again in the living room, Maria refused the wine. She needed her wits. The strain of the gathering was getting on her nerves, and she kept looking for openings to get away. But Sal and John kept things going well into the evening.

Maria was dying to return to her apartment, but Ariel had told her to take it slowly. It was John who got up to leave first.

"Stop lookin' at your watch," Sal said to Maria. "And wait a minute, John; I have somethin' to say before you leave."

Sal went to the bedroom, and returned with an oversized envelope. He pulled out a receipt.

"Four reservations for the Rainbow Room in New York for next Friday night, the New Age celebration. Dinner and dancin'."

"Dad, I'm busy," said Maria.

"Doin' what? Everyone's talkin' this up. It's bigger than any New Year celebration and it's our Mayan heritage."

"Dad you don't still believe that stuff?"

"I don' know, I heard it soo much in the old days."

"Tell us, "said Maria, wanting some background in case the angel asked. Besides, it would pass for conversation.

"Well, as far as I can remember from what the shamans said..." and he was off on the story.

Sal told of the Long Count, the 5,000 year cycles, Gucumatz the Creator, Zipacna the Demon. How the Gods formed the Earth in the 1st World but set no humans upon it, letting it float in an azure sea. So they created the 2nd World of animals and people. But the people they made of mud and they crumbled and washed away, and the animals ignored the Gods and squawked and howled and could not worship them. They banished these to the forests and made the monkeys howl for all time. Then they tried a 3rd time and made man of wood but he had no soul and forgot who had made him so the Gods rained down a black resin that covered the humans and suffocated them, forcing those few who survived down into the UnderWorld turning them into demons. Finally, the Gods made man from maize, the beloved corn, and he was good. He fought the demons and worshiped the Gods like he should. And now the 5th World was coming and no one knew what it would bring, but many thought the UnderWorld would release the demons so they could control the next World.

"So, can you make it?" asked Sal.

"Well, I don't know just yet."

"How busy could you be?" asked Rosa. "Your father has wanted this for years. To be someplace special when we start the next world. Do you know how much these reservations cost?"

"Six thousand dollars," said John.

"How do you know?" asked Sal.

"I read about it in Time. This 5th World event is worldwide. I should have drawn something for it."

"Well, anyway, I have the tickets and we like you two to join us."

John sat silent.

"Oh, we pay for the hotel and the flights. All you have to do is come," said Sal.

"I don't know," said Maria. "If you knew how busy I was..."

"I need your answers by Monday, otherwise we ask the Logans."

"I can tell you by then," said Maria.

"Listen, Sal," began John. "It's very generous of you, but..."

"By Monday?" said Sal.

"Okay."

It was time to leave. Maria and John exchanged pleasantries.

"Don' disappoint your father," Rosa whispered in Maria's ear at the door. "You know how hard he worked for his money, sendin' you to school and things. Now he wants to do this. You know he never asks…"

Out on the porch, as Rosa watched from behind the blinds, John asked Maria, "Are you alright?"

"I'm not interested in any performances in front of my parents."

"Stop taking yourself so seriously. You're as tight as a tick."

"There's a lot going on at work."

"There always was."

"Unlike with you."

"If you think I'd ever want back with you, Mein Fuhrer, you're delusional."

"Let's not start. Of course you know I won't be going to New York."

"Me neither. It's just hard to say no to Sal."

"I know, he asks for so little. Maybe next year."

John stepped off the porch first. "Take care, Maria," he said.

"You, too."

Maria watched him go to his car.

During the drive back home, Maria again thought about how crazy all this was. Yet it was an opportunity beyond her wildest expectations. An angel telling her she had been chosen to save mankind, that she alone could build the device needed to protect man from evil. What a trip! Now she had to drop all her plans for a week, and focus like she had never focused before. A rush ran down her spine. She hoped she wasn't still dreaming. She wanted this more than anything. She parked in her slot and opened the door to her apartment.

The contrast between Maria's place and Elaine's was extreme. The light rug, white sofa and chairs, gleaming chrome and brass, all as perfectly in place as her decorator and maid could make it. The clean work area, frosted light wall behind her monitor, smell of cleanser in the air. The only flaws were the finger marks on the light switch. She'd talk to the maid about that. She walked into the kitchen.

Ariel was there.

Maria gasped, "You don't look like an angel."

"We are not the creatures in your greeting cards," said Ariel.

"I'm a little confused," continued Maria. "What happens after I make the device you want? How will it be used? What will it do?"

"Everything in its time," said the angel. "You will always know enough to proceed."

"But I prefer to work with all the parameters in hand. Do you trust me or don't you?"

"Our trust is complete. You need to show patience. I am but a conduit of the Lord's wish. No one should question Him."

"Another reason I don't believe most of that stuff."

But Maria didn't need belief for this. She'd even fake it for something so important. She had to keep Ariel happy.

"Can you at least lay out the timing for me?" said Maria.

"You will have the time and you will have the equipment; that is my role. Know that I am guiding you even when I am not visible."

"I'm having a problem with this."

"Maria, you are rational. If I am wrong you will have lost one week from your life. If I am correct you will have done a service beyond the grasp of any human."

"Oh, Christ," thought Maria.

Ariel raised an eyebrow.

"Sorry, I was just thinking."

"You must know that evil forces are loose and can be very persuasive. I cannot even be sure of my cohorts. They listened to The Dark One before and may again."

"We're in a race?"

"Yes. Others will try to duplicate your work, or try to stop you, or place false friends in your midst."

"How can I know who to trust?"

"Heed me."

Then the angel was gone.

"It isn't fair," thought Maria. "Ariel comes and goes with pieces of the plan and I have to wait for her to show up again." She had never worked in such a fog before. She went into the bathroom and looked at herself. She needed sleep, if that were possible. Tomorrow would be a busy day. She forgot about brushing her teeth, went to the unmade bed, and pulled up the covers.

At 1:30 AM the phone rang. Maria knocked the receiver off with her arm, it fell to the floor. She picked it up and said, "Hello?"

"What was that?" asked Elaine.

"I dropped the phone. What time is it?"

"Late. Listen. I'm scared."

"Of what?"

"I just dreamed, or hallucinated, that I was being tortured."

"Elaine! You're not starting again?"

"I just dropped some Ecstasy, to celebrate the job. I don't know if it put me out or not, because it seemed so real."

"Who was torturing you?"

"Weird things, like evil gnomes, and a voice shouting, 'Shun her. Shun her!'"

"You should know better than to use that stuff. I thought I could rely on you."

"You can, you can! I won't do any more. I just had to tell someone about this."

"Should I come over?"

"No, I'm okay. Maybe I was subconsciously worried about your 'secret' contacts."

"Elaine, these contacts only do good. I'm sure we'll both know more in a few days."

4

Early Sunday Morning
December 16th

Maria lay in bed sifting through the events of the last 24 hours. Doubt, an emotion foreign to her, spread to her consciousness, signaling Ariel.

"Why me?" asked Maria.

Ariel said, "We need your strength, your single-mindedness."

"You've told me that already, but there must be others who could do this."

"No, Maria, you have been chosen for a reason."

"Which is?"

Ariel reminded Maria again of her thesis topic, "Programmatic Control of Worldwide Video Terminals by Web/Field Interactions."

"Only you can make it come to life," Ariel said.

"But I wrote that years ago, and it was just theoretical. I'm not sure any of the calculations I made yesterday would stand up in a real trial."

"That is why we will test it."

Maria needed to get control of herself. Her ambition always pushed her to accept promotions, even when they drew her away from the lab. She'd rationalize that, with more workers under her, she'd make more progress. She scoffed at John's warning: "Artists build a small artificial world they can entirely control - scientists work with the real world. It's too big, too complex for complete control."

But Ariel offered a simple and elegant solution to a momentous problem, and Maria was the only person who could pull it off. Giving angels simultaneous direct access to the whole world would bring peace. People needed to be told how to behave.

"Evil dominates man," said Ariel. "The true path has to be shown to them directly, in a way that will convince them completely."

The program Maria had written at Caltech could control the output of any video screen, and, most importantly for this mission, access any terminal that was plugged into an electrical outlet or had an installed battery, all from one remote site. The computing power to do this had not been available then – not even to the military. What it could be used for was anyone's guess, and - as she had told Elaine - it was illegal. So the thesis sat buried in the stacks at the Millikan library, forgotten by everyone, including Maria.

"I can give you the opportunity to realize your research," Ariel said. "You must remember praying for that then?"

"I've never prayed for anything since I was a little girl."

"We hear your prayers, whether formal or not."

Maria looked away.

"Remember how thrilled you were when your theory worked out? That little demonstration? Do you want to show others what you conceived? You will be the peacemaker of the world. We seek no recognition; the glory will attend to you alone."

"Sure, that's exciting for me, but what will this do for you?"

"The Next World approaches," said the angel.

"So?"

"Have you forgotten what John wrote in the Apocalypse?

> *And I saw an angel come down from heaven, having the key of the bottomless pit and a great chain in his hand. And he laid hold on the…Devil, and bound him a thousand years…and set a seal upon him, that he should deceive the nations no more…And when the thousand years are expired, Satan shall be loosed from his prison…"*

"No one believes that stuff, and, besides, that was for the Millennium" said Maria.

"It is the word of the Lord; your current human dates are meaningless. The cosmic cycles are set. The ancients knew this," said Ariel.

"Sounds more like John was on drugs."

"Maria, I know you mean well, I can see your heart, but do not mock the scriptures."

"Are you serious?"

"Of course. The Devil has been bound in hell for each cycle and only has his minions to do his bidding on the Earth. But when this 4th World ends, Satan himself will be freed, and his full power will be unleashed into the world. If he is not conquered and bound again, the world will end."

"Sure, the 4th World. So you are Mayan?" Asked Maria.

"All civilizations intersect. On Earth, in Heaven," said the angel.

"What will Satan do?"

"The Devil knows that for humans, images are reality. Your 'Seeing is believing – *veni, vidi, vici.*'"

"The Fiend will show humans despair. The final sin," said Ariel.

She described how the Global Village could not watch looting, killing, and catastrophic chaos without spiraling into hopelessness. If the Devil controls the visual, he will control the world. If humans see him working his evil before their programmed eyes they will believe he has won. Perception is everything; that is why the good have to control the Devil's access and cut off his plans.

"So Friday night is the end of the world?"

"As you know it. Unless you help us contain him."

"Why doesn't God contain him?"

"It is not ours to question the ways of the Lord, Maria. It is sufficient for us to know that it is man's duty to fight this battle. The Holy One waits for you to choose, then sends us to battle beside you."

"Why didn't the world end 5,000 years ago, or 5,000 years before that, or even earlier? Is it a coincidence that the pyramids are 5000 years old," asked Maria?"

"There are no coincidences, child."

Ariel said it was forbidden for her to describe the battles of former times, when men and angels warred with the demons and subdued them again. She told Maria that the cleft above her upper lip ("What you call Cupid's bow or the philtrum," she said) was formed when her soul was leaving heaven. Ariel put it there to set in Maria's unconscious the need to seal her lips from telling about the glory of the place she was leaving, the many wonders of God and his angels, and to help her forget the grandeur that awaited her return.

"You have forgotten, as you should have."

But now mankind had progressed to a dangerous point. No longer did the forces of evil have to fight many battles, all over the Earth. Man had given Satan the power to reach the farthest corners of the Earth simultaneously. The power of mass communication is man's Achilles heel. Nations consolidated their communications networks to gain control of the population. Their different secret access codes to protect their webs will be the avenue for the wicked, if Ariel did not get there first.

"They will control the message and the messenger," said Ariel. "The Devil will mesmerize the people with his guile, leading them to sin and pleasure while his host destroys them."

"How can I fight against the Devil?"

"What you build, with our guidance, will give us the means to stop his transmission. We will control the terminals, not him. We will broadcast peace, not war. Unable to contact man, Satan will have to fight us without human help. We will defeat him."

"What if I fail?"

"You must not fail. Did Abraham fail? Moses? Joshua? Peter?"

"You put me in that company?"

"Why not? They were human, like you. They were given a great deed to fulfill and they did it. Do you think they acted alone?"

"Well..."

And Ariel was gone again.

5

Larry lived entirely within the confines of his video screen. He barely spoke to anyone at work, ate alone, only answered e-mail; lived in his electronic village. It would be kind to call him pudgy. His girth came not from overeating, but from inactivity. The only parts that got exercise were his hands, eyes, and brain. His first 24 years were aimless, except that 16 of them involved a computer. Then MicroFrame found him, and gave him 11 years of bliss, so far.

And it was getting better. While everyone else had worked on competitors for the Pentium, the higher P series, and specialty chips for limited use, Larry had been given the freedom to devise a new breakthrough processor.

"Forget backward compatibility," said his boss. "You give us a processor that zooms from the ground up. We want to move peta-gobs of data onto the GlobeNet at speeds limited only by signal velocity."

For the last seven years it was all Larry had done. He scrapped the old architecture, used the newest semiconductors, shunted mundane calculations to auxiliary chips, and built the Excalibur. Debugging it took Larry a while, but except for a few floating errors it was ready for beta testing. The lab was behind in designing the rest of the circuit.

This was of little concern to Larry. The longer the Excalibur was his alone, the happier he was. Delays on the consumer side meant more time for him to play with his baby. Sometimes he would just rotate the chip in his fingers, looking at it from all sides. It was a marvelous sight for someone who understood its perfection.

Nothing but work pleased him. Larry disliked his apartment; it meant he wasn't at work with his machines. So he rigged set-ups that transformed his home into an extension of his workbench. He walked into the kitchen area, turned on the kitchen computer, scrolled down to select a menu, picked braised beef, and hit *enter*. When the meal was ready, he placed it on a stiff paper plate, took it to the living area, and logged onto the Net. He operated the mouse with his left hand so he could use his right to eat as he surfed. He barely noticed the taste of the food.

Dinner's over, it's playtime! Larry went to the bedroom closet, removed the shoe box, and took out a cylinder ten inches long. He opened that and shook out the sleeve. Returning to the living room computer, he raised the keyboard platform, took off his pants, and sat down.

First he backed the chair away from the desk, slid the neoprene and spandex tube over his penis, and connected the wire chassis to the computer. Then he adjusted the sheath taut at the base, slid the rubber hood over his scrotum, strapped the belt attached to the hood back over the top of his penis, cinched the whole thing tight, and checked to see it was secure.

256 sensors ran from the sheath to the wire cable. That was connected to a transfer box that interfaced with the multi-phase DVD. Larry placed a fragrance helmet on his head, and pulled the side bar near his nose. In place of a monitor, Larry had a plasma board that could be tilted to any angle, like an architect's desk. The screen was 4x6 feet with voice input. The mixture of liquid crystals added a third dimension to the view. Larry slid his right hand into a visualizer glove and touched "stylus."

He selected the "Girls With Attitudes" disc from the DVD collection he had purchased by mail from "PC Games" magazine, clicked on "select type," chose "willing and able," scrolled down to "Linda," and touched "start."

Linda strutted onto the screen from the left, all 640,000,000 pixels of her. She was dressed in high-class hooker fashion: long legs, pedestaled atop 6" heels, short leather mini-skirt, wide belt cinched at her waist, silky cream blouse above, long gloves, choker around her neck, Beyoncé hair, thick lipstick, and, a detail added by Larry, librarian eyeglasses.

When she got to the middle of the screen, she turned, faced front, and said, "Hello, Larry."

"Hello, Linda," he replied.

Just the sound of her voice started him off; it layered over her poses and gestures (the real turn-on) that were programmed to send signals down to the sensors anchored in the sheath. If she thrust her hips forward the sensors around the head of his penis vibrated. If she played with herself the sensors along the length heated up. If she said what she wanted to do to him while pointing to the spot she wanted filled, all the sensors directly stimulated his nerve endings. His arousal spread; so did the sheath.

Larry answered her every question.

"Do you want me?" she breathed.

"Oh, yes."

"Can you handle a number as hot as me?"

"Yes."

The smell of her lipstick and perfume wafted up his nose.

"Let's see you start some action."

Larry put his hand on the plasma screen, near Linda's waist.

"Is that all you can touch?"

He moved up to her breast, rubbing the glove slowly over her blouse.

"Hmmm. I like it like that. Do it some more."

Her figure moved in response to his hand.

"Lower, lower," she panted.

He moved his hand to her crotch, pheromones filling his nostrils.

"Oh, touch me again there, harder."

Larry stretched his fingers; a feeling of control moved up his arm.

Linda knew her stuff. She pranced, strutted, minced, and cooed, every gesture getting Larry closer. Tonight, Larry had the sheath programmed for extended teasing, always numbing down when it reached a certain size. A random generator determined how long this would last before the override clicked in and both the sheath and Linda went wild on him. This uncertainty kept Larry guessing, wanting both more teasing and relief.

He felt the sweat building up in the glove and down inside the sheath. Linda rolled and undulated, controlling the motion of Larry's hand. He started breathing harder. Now he was smelling poon-tang.

"Oh, oh, talk to me, lover."

"Linda, you're so beautiful, so sexy, so mine," he said.

Twenty-three minutes into the program it happened. Larry's eyes were glued to the screen, his pelvis bouncing off the chair, his hand gripping the table. Now the sheath seemed to have a mind of its own. Short of pulling the plug, Larry was no longer in control. Linda was moaning, her legs open and spread toward the screen; she bucked and shouted for Larry to hurry. His breath came in puffs, his skin flushed, and he exploded into the sheath.

"More, more, lover. Do it to me. Don't stop," she said, as she milked him to exhaustion. He could smell her sweat.

Larry sat there in a trance. Linda said, "When will I see you again?"

Larry's lips, barely able to move, said, "Tomorrow."

"Okay, Lover Boy," Linda said, and glided off the screen to the right, blowing him a kiss from her pursed lips.

Larry thought of marketing the device, but really wasn't interested in sharing his fun with anyone. Let the others be satisfied with their flesh and blood lovers, Larry had better. What real girl could compete with his harem? And it was safe sex.

Miranda was different. She met Larry on Friday when their cars collided in the parking lot of the 7-Eleven. He was stunned by her beauty, beyond that of the best girl on any computer. She insisted he give her his address so she could help pay for the damages, which she blamed on herself. To his shock, she appeared at his apartment door that night.

"You can't come in, this place is a mess."

"I don't care, Larry," she said. "Please, you must let me in."

More scared than interested, Larry opened the door. His reaction was new to him. No real girl, however pretty, had caused him to get hard so fast. He was confused. Miranda seemed to like him. He gave into her quickly and completely, like a puppy on a chain.

And when it was over, she did not intrude into his affairs, other than sexual. He liked that. She didn't insist on cleaning his house, asking him to bathe, wanting to go places. No, she just came over and humped his eyes out. Friday was the best night he had ever had, and then again Saturday, the best day he ever had. He came six times in 9 hours. Sunday was the first time Larry thought about work again. He wanted to stay with Miranda, but she told him to go to work and she would come back that evening.

Back at MicroFrame, Larry, one of the few in the building on Sunday, was completing his last chores. It was 7:15 PM, and the place was almost empty. Miranda appeared in his office.

"How did you get past security?"

"I asked to see you."

"But they would have called up here first."

Before he could speak again, her lips were glued to his. Then his pants were down, and they were having at it in the room Larry treasured most. When it was over, Larry was spent, pliable, wanting to rest.

"I need you to get me something," said Miranda.

"Anything!"

"Three Excalibur chips."

Larry was startled. Excalibur was just a rumor, even inside MicroFrame. Larry had the chips, of course, but give them away? Even to Miranda?

"But those chips are worthless to anyone but me. If our competition found them in a parking lot they wouldn't know what to do with them."

"Oh, Larry, won't you do this for me? Please?"

"You're a spy for the competition."

"No, I promise, honey, no other company will see them," she said.

For the first time in his adult life, Larry trusted someone. He just knew Miranda wouldn't harm him.

"But why do you even want one? They're only in the experimental stage."

"I can be of help to you if you let me. There's an error in them you don't even know about. I have friends who can fix it."

"Tell me more," he asked and she did, much more.

"I promise I'll tell you everything else next week."

Again, for some unknown reason, this seemed logical to Larry. She really appeared to know others who might help with details that were useful but of less interest to him. Why bother with that crap anyway? Let them clean up in the corners so he could concentrate more on the power loads. They couldn't fathom the algorithms only he knew.

He went to the security cabinet and entered his password. The door clicked open and he reached inside, pulled out a small unmarked box, and raised its lid. The box had a series of 64 metal holders, 29 of which held processors. Larry pulled out three, closed the lid, put the box back, and secured the cabinet.

"Let me mark these so I know they're the ones you took," he said.

"See you later," she said. "I know a way out so they won't detect the chips."

"But you said you told the guard..."

She was gone before he could ask any more.

Larry was confused, so he got his stuff together and left. He didn't ask the guard anything; he just wanted to get home.

And, sure enough, Miranda came over later and they were humping like hyenas.

6

Sunday, December 16th
10:15 AM EST

Dave Selby reached over his head and shut off the alarm. It was still dark out, but he preferred an early start, a good afternoon nap, and a late ending to his days. He liked freelancing better than his old position as a "scout" for a processor company. This way he worked when he liked, although that seemed more frequent now with all the new competition lowering prices.

He logged onto the Net.

From: M^3@gmail.com
To: chipscout@aol.com
Subj: analysis
Date: 16 Dec 2012 8:15 AM (EST)

This is Maria. Sorry for the early request, but I need to interface with you ASAP. I have reason to prefer a secure line. Can you mail back if you're available this morning? Please use a public line. My encrypted number is 412-857-3341, play it forward.

Dave sat back in his chair. Maria Montez wanting a secure transmission? How could Miss Goody-Two-Shoes be in any trouble? He got dressed, went to the local hotel, plugged into one of the phone lines at the back of the lobby, rang the number, then mailed back.

The phone in the Burger King rang once; Maria looked at her screen.

From: chipscout@aol.com
To: M³@gmail.com
Subj: reply analysis
Date: 16 Dec 2012 7:45 AM (PCT)
I'm assuming this is Maria Montez, am I correct?

From: M³@gmail.com
To: chipscout@aol.com
Subj: talk
Date: 16 Dec 2012 10:50 AM (EST)
This is Maria. I use my exponential name for secrecy. You know anything I transmit under my regular handle is being monitored by the company. Can we go IRT and chat?

From: chipscout@aol.com
To: M³@aol.com
Subj: reply talk
Date: 16 Dec 2012 07:52 AM (PCT)
Sure. You're lucky I check my mail the first thing when I get up. What are we having here, portables and public lines? Just in

case we get lost, work out 408-562-7071 and call me. I'll wait for your prompt.

From: M³@gmail.com
To: chipscout@aol.com
Subj: chat
Date: 16 Dec 2012 10:55 AM (EST)
Good, we can talk. You know the most "secure" account is a public one. By the time anyone tried to sift through the hundreds of millions on-line, I'll be home free.

<What trouble are you in?
>Trust me - no trouble. I just need to do something a little unusual, that's all.
<Then I'm your man. What's the ticket?
>For reasons I'm not even sure of, I have to scope a chip that hasn't been released yet. Your description of how to do that (which you told me at the last CAPSTAL meeting) didn't register because I had no interest. I have interest now. I need to know what traps are in the fabricated product to stop thieves. Please send me the details if you have them available.
<I can tell you what I know and what the valley talk is saying. But you have to let me know what level chip you are talking about. The more sophisticated ones require a different approach. BTW I thought you guys bought all yours?
>Not always. This one is top level, beyond anything out there less than a SuperCray, and it's not for sale yet. No backward compatibility even.
<Look, this is my business. You're talking about an Excalibur aren't you? And if you think you can scope that, I suggest the old-fashioned method, bribe someone.
>Please don't ask me any more details; I'm at risk just talking to anyone.
<OK, I'm in. Tell me more.
>Suppose it was an Excalibur? How would I scope out the architecture?

< Let me start from the top. Sometimes the package is the best line of defense. They'd have begun with terbium-doped silica fiber-optic lines spaghetti layered to foil removal. The only way to circumvent those would be with secondary emission imaging. Assuming you got by that, you'd have to deactivate the sapphire bundles put into the plastic. Hit one of those land mines and the chip is destroyed. You know more about how focused pulsed lasers can get around these than I do, so good hunting. With me so far?

> Fine. References on the sapphire loading?

< I'll download references for everything at the end of this transmission. You can print out what you need. After peeling through those two traps you'll have to contend with passive metal layering that shields the lower levels from electron beam scrutiny. That's possible with a sensing magnet. Then you'll be down to the chip surface, and you can use HRMP and VCEM to analyze the internal states. Think of it as etching away a finite number of layers. Still there?

> Yes. How fast could this be done?

< Hold on, KemoSabe. All this is for naught unless you can read the operating conditions and image the internal states while the chip is powered. A few side routes or some buried feeder lines could cause you to make a mistake and burn out. That's where an electron probe comes in handy. A thorough analysis could be done in a few hours, even quicker with the right equipment in the right hands.

> Great! So that's it?

< No. The most important element is next - LUCK!

> Thanks, David. I'm buying next meeting.

< When can you tell me what you're really up to?

> I'll call you in a week.

7

Sunday, December 16
1 PM

Maria had her instructions. The calm Ariel instilled didn't override her drive to start the project and get on with the test run. Her mind was spinning, racing through the decisions she would face. There could be no mistakes; she had to plan correctly from the start if she was to get everything done in time. This was more intimidating than her PhD orals and all of her project presentations at Infinity combined.

She went into the kitchen, made some cranberry tea, and returned to the living room. The figure on the couch startled her.

"Oh, my God!"

The man was big, over six feet, handsome in a frightening way, stern yet approachable.

Maria wasn't going to ask this one anything.

"I am Michael," he said. "I have come to save you."

"I'm being saved already," said Maria.

"So you have been told. But you are in the hold of demons."

"What demons? No one gets me to do anything I don't want to do."

"The sure, the conceited, are easily manipulated. And you crave power."

"Don't try talking down to me. I'm not one of your believers."

"Another reason you were selected."

"Look, if you have a problem we can take it up when Ariel returns."

"Ariel? He's calling himself Ariel?"

"She is."

"We call him 'The Resister,' 'Satan,' or 'The Slanderer,' 'Devil.'"

"Ariel warned me about you."

"And did he tell you you were doing God's work?"

"I want you to leave."

"I am not here for your wants, but to deliver you from evil."

"Ariel is not evil. She is beautiful. She knows everything that will happen and has picked me to save the world."

"Flattery, the sin of pride, his sin. The evil I am here to save you from is in you. If you ally yourself with 'The Destroyer,' you will aid the annihilation of your kind."

"I've the skills she needs to stop demons like you from destroying the world."

"The demons have the world. This is where they were cast. We control them through human goodness. Together we keep them at bay."

"Then why are you worried about me?"

"You know much but understand little. You are under a spell, and it is the time."

"What time?"

"When Satan was cast down, and bound in the pit, it was determined that he be loosed when the celestial clock turns so that the forces of good may prove themselves worthy by binding him again."

"Every thousand years?" Maria played dumb.

Michael explained the history. When mankind was fully created in the 4th World, God was pleased. He gave man lust, allowed him to be tempted, so that he could overcome sin and prove himself worthy through free will. Angels were God's messengers to man. But Satan grew jealous of man. He saw that God loved the Earth and its people, and he knew that by being tested those people would come closer to God than he. So, he tempted Eve to disobey God, to learn the knowledge God forbade her. Eve resisted, but the Evil One was cunning and knew how to sway her, promising she would be "like God." When Eve took the fruit from the Tree of Knowledge, she experienced sin.

When Adam joined her he felt unclean also. They covered their nakedness. For their transgression they were cast from the Garden, into a world full of demons. They would know death.

Satan was brought before the Holy One and was cast down to the place man calls Hell. From there he tries to rule the world. Mankind, through his goodness, fights the demons the Devil unleashes each day, and sometimes wins.

"Why did Satan turn from God?" asked Maria.

"At the heart of Satan's choice lies the mystery of evil," said Michael.

"Why are we more threatened now?"

"Every cycle, Satan is unbound from the depths and can overcome man. Only through the intercession of angels, at war with evil, can man win his place again and throw the Devil back into the frozen lake and the fiery pit," said Michael.

"Ariel has told me most of this."

"As he would, to gain your confidence."

"Now you want me to believe your version instead?"

"Yes, Maria."

"Then tell me of the previous wars."

Michael went on. He told of the time eons ago when God sent pestilence to the earth to warn man and to prepare him for the battle to come. Demons had used foreign armies to take the holy places; men turned from God and worshipped Mammon; the poor wallowed in sin, using their misery as an excuse to deny Him. False idols were set-up; devils spoke through the mouths of oracles; man turned his attention inward and looked for worthiness in the basest of things. The Dark One was pleased.

When the time came, Satan was unleashed. He roamed the world, happy at the sight of human depravation. Victory was at his hand.

But then man repented. Prophets arose who preached the Good Way. They warned the people that they must fight evil to win redemption. After great effort, mankind listened to them and fought back. Then the angels were able to assist them as God provides. Together they slew the demons and their cohorts, turning the wayward into the chosen ones again. Satan fought a mighty battle, but lost. Man rested, exhausted.

God, pleased again with man, saw that humans had been weakened by the relentless wars. He sent The Redeemer, His Son, The Messiah, to the Earth to strengthen them.

"You mean Jesus came to rescue us?"

"No," explained Michael. "Mankind had won the war, but needed help to attain the state of grace he had lost. He would not survive the next war without a period of rebuilding his faith. Only through worship and sacrifice would man regain the strength to fight again. So Jesus ministered to His people and they thrived. The sacrifices of martyrs spread the faith throughout the world."

"What about the other times?"

"Yes, so long ago. People again despaired. Some saw in the Scriptures the portent of annihilation, The Number of the Beast-666-turned upside down, the thousandth year from Christ's birth. But few understood the number and fewer realized its importance. Your Mayan ancestors calculated correctly.

"They were not even Catholic."

"Do you forget Baptism of Desire? Do you think God leaves good people without salvation? All the world and all its people are God's. How could it be otherwise? The route to Him is goodness."

When the battle was joined, Satan, was prepared.

"He sent out legions of devils, led by his cohort Beelzebub, to start the process of death throughout the world. They fought against all people, in many battles. Your Mayan ancestors saw the onslaught of the cave dwellers, powerful men controlled by demons. They covered the land where your people lived, raping women, killing men, destroying everyone and everything in their path. Those who survived were enslaved.

"Then men of religion, leaders, sprang up to defend the faith. In your ancestral land, Ekchuah rallied the poor slaves and fought. Day after day he prayed in his war tent and we guided him. He drove the demons into the sea, and slaughtered them in the water. When he was through he raised his sword to heaven and proclaimed his undying praise to the Lord. A remnant of the defeated came upon Ekchuah in his sleep and slew him. But from his seed sprang others who continued the process by which man returned to the faith. That happened all over the world, and the earth was safe for another cycle. And now a Great Cycle approaches and with it a great choice," he said.

Maria was confused, "You tell a good story, tempting to believe. It almost makes sense, just the way a demon's story would. But you have no solution. Ariel knows humans must help her and she has given me the chance to participate. You offer nothing. Why would I listen to you? I will resist you as I would resist any evil."

"Ha! What evil have you ever resisted with your conceit? Do you honor your parents? Do you covet? You have to return to your faith, humble yourself," said Michael. "Only then will you gain control. Only then will you know who is speaking the truth."

"Get out!"

Michael looked at Maria, a stare that held neither contempt nor pity.

"I will grant you your wish for the moment," he said.

Michael rose from the couch and floated above the startled woman. His human clothes melted and his body transformed its shape. His trunk thickened; feathers appeared along the side. His legs lengthened, the muscles tensed like coiled steel cables under his skin; he spread out his arms, the strength evident in the powerful way he grasped a sword with his right hand.

"I am an Archangel," he said.

His feet were set in flat sandals, bare except for the bands that circled his instep and ankle. Above these were garters of metal, each ringed with a silver band. His skirt was of burnished brass, pleated in strong folds; the girdle around his waist was cinched tight, on it the inscription "Prince of the Heavenly Host." His breastplate was pewter, with rows of stars across its middle; his collar dark leather, with silver spikes jutting out. He had the look of a warrior, a commander, the leader of the celestial army. Atop his head was a shock of golden hair, curls falling down to frame his strong face. Above his powerful wings was a scarlet cloak, waving in the wind, the ends trailing behind. A sash fitted over his shoulder, embroidered with gold. His stance was challenging, as if he were waiting, primed for battle.

Then Michael pulled the great sword from its scabbard and shouted.

"It was I who liberated Peter from the cell, saved Daniel from the beasts, stopped Abraham from killing his only son. With Gabriel I spoke to Muhammad. I defeated the Archfiend, subjugated him, cast him to the pit as my Lord commanded. I guard not just you, but all mankind. Heed my warning!"

Maria backed away.

Michael rose farther, the ceiling gone and only a vast emptiness above. He turned so that he was facing down and looked at Maria. Then he shot up and away, quicker than Maria thought possible. In the distance he was no larger than a Christmas tree bulb - and he disappeared, like a bulb burning out. The sudden loss startled Maria. She was alone again.

A wind entered from above, forcing her to the floor. Then a voice said, "If you deny me you will suffer the loss of Cain."

"Ariel, help me," Maria pleaded. There was no response. She wanted to call the whole thing off, to tell Ariel to find someone stronger, to pass this chalice to another.

But nothing happened, nothing changed.

8

Sunday, 3:00 PM

"Tricks," said Ariel. "No more than your magicians do. His guile is man's fall. He is not the Michael you are thinking of."

"I guess you're right," said Maria, "but how can I know?"

"Did he show you how he tempted our Lord Jesus in the desert? Offering Him food and glory, chiding Him to perform miracles?"

"No, but he made me doubt you."

"His first temptation. Eve too had doubts. You should look into your heart."

"But I need proof," said Maria.

"Proof? Where would mankind be if we had to prove ourselves to you? Did Job not suffer without proof? Was Peter always sure? Did Augustine not have doubts?"

"But I'm not a saint, I need more."

"This is most irregular."

"Irregular? I was fine before you came, now I'm in a state of - what - hallucination? You're asking me to do something that's never been done before. And you say if I don't do it the world will be destroyed!"

"Maria, you were not that fine before I came. Remember that Mary had doubts too, but, in the end, she followed the angel."

"I'm not Mary either!"

"Sit down and calm yourself."

"Calm? First you come, then another wondrous being says I should not listen to you. How am I to know who to believe?"

"God will direct your choice."

"Take me to see Him."

"That is not possible. If you want me to prove anything to you, you must allow me to do it my way. Angels have rules, too."

"I have to have something."

"If you insist, I will give you a vision you will not forget."

Maria sat still. Her eyes got heavy, the lids closed. She felt a slight tremor run up her spine and leave from the top of her head. Then it happened.

Maria's eyes slammed open. She was with Ariel, in a space unlike anything she had ever seen. All around was a dark cobalt blue, a harsh breeze, an eerie sound, like the yawning of a great reptile. Ariel was holding Maria by the waist. Neither spoke.

After some time, Ariel alighted on a precipice, then slowly slid her hand over Maria's eyes. When she removed it, Maria looked down.

In front of her an enormous stone gate stood open, the inscription above reading, "Abandon Every Hope, All Ye Who Enter Here."

Maria had never seen a blackness like the one that surrounded the scenes inside the gate. Blood red flames licked up toward the spot where they stood, sulfurous smells filled the air, anguished cries pierced her ears.

As far as Maria could see, people were trapped in the abyss below. Some were covered with open sores, others had no skin, a few glowed from cinders under their flesh. The smell of burning flesh caused Maria to retch, clutching her stomach as the vomit spewed out. Ariel waited, then pointed ahead

People in pits were attended by devils, each with long spikes. When they screamed, the devils thrust the spikes down their throats. One devil was pouring a thick liquid over the souls in his pit. It inflamed their skin and entered their mouths when they wailed. In another pit demons were beating people with lashes of green metal, opening wide sores. Other demons threw hot coals into the new sores. The shrieks shook Maria's body.

Maria saw the famous, tormented by the knowledge that their sins had brought them this despair. Salome, Paris, Helen of Troy, Don Juan, all the lustful, were arrayed in beautiful clothes, each desiring the other, kept apart by invisible barriers, like birds in imaginary cages. The gluttons, Henry VIII, Cleopatra, Carnegie, were forced to eat muck unendingly. Those who had committed suicide, like Judas, were kept as pure souls in a sealed bottle, looking out at the bodies they had denied, now denied to them. Deceivers, whores, pimps, all sinners, were racked with the knowledge of eternal damnation.

A steady stream of people entered the pits from the west.

"The newly damned," said Ariel.

Maria watched them being clawed and prodded, barely able to walk. A look of utter despair covered their faces. If one stumbled, he or she was hurled upward and dropped into the middle of a churning lake.

"Look there," said Ariel.

Maria followed Ariel's finger. There in the distance was the palace of Pandemonium and within it a throne, and on that an enormous figure, all black and red, his long nails scraped the ground; his leathery wings covered the seat. He looked at Maria; opened his mouth, and spewed forth a vile laugh. The sound reverberated throughout Hell, turning all faces toward it.

Then the figure spoke, "Your world believes only what it sees and by vision we will control you. You have boxed your input onto video screens and through them you are ours."

"I've seen enough!" Maria screamed.

"Not yet."

Ariel motioned for Maria to follow. They came down the hill to the river Styx. Charon, the boatman, carried them over to a pit of brimstone. Maria looked down and saw the faces of some of her relatives and neighbors who had died. But one face shocked her most. Here was Doris Gleason, her best friend, who had died in an auto accident, screaming for Maria to help her.

Maria glanced at Ariel.

"Of course you cannot intervene," said the angel.

"No?" shouted Maria. "Then take me away. Bring me back to earth!"

But Ariel had more. She flew Maria away from Hell, away from the smells, away from the damned souls. They were back in the cobalt space, the bracing wind again in their faces.

All at once they hurled through an opening and into brightness.

"Wait, Maria, your eyes will adapt."

When she could see again, Maria was stunned. Here was a realm of light, faint purple and gold, shining from the horizon to the spot where she stood with Ariel.

"I imagined it would be like this," said Maria.

"No one imagines the totality," said Ariel.

And the angel was right. Maria now saw a host of angels, arranged in concentric circles, some on the clouds in front, some in the heavens above. They were not moving, not floating either; they were just there. And they were singing. Maria had never heard such sweet sounds. The voices were clear and soft, the accompaniment low yet penetrating. The sounds were directed toward a gilded throne set in the middle of the space. On the throne was a bright light.

"God," said Ariel. "But you are not worthy to see him yet."

Above the chair another light shone and to God's right still another.

"The Trinity," said Ariel. "You will understand when you are rewarded in the afterlife."

"Can we get closer?"

"No. I am at risk taking you this far. Had your mission been less important I would have left you when you doubted me."

"I don't doubt you now, Ariel. May we stay here?"

Ariel told her of wonders that she could not yet see. Of the orders of angels and how they attended God. Of the souls of the blessed and their higher place because they had overcome sin and attained Heaven. She spoke of the Anointed Ones, those closest to God, of the Dominations, the elect of God, of the Thrones, His closest attendants, of the Seraphim, God's choir.

Maria's aching mind was healing. She felt the peace of the place and a desire to make that peace her own. She asked again to remain.

"No, Maria. Your life's work is unfinished. You must complete it before you can ask for this. But when you truly ask, He will grant it to you. We must leave now so you can assume your mortal shell."

"Why is it all Christian? I thought everyone could be saved."

"You see it through the lens of what you've been taught, child. The reality is total."

Ariel picked her up and held her toward the light. They slowly receded, the heavenly host becoming smaller as they backed away; the singing faint, inaudible. The cobalt sky again.

They came back to the living room and sat a while. Then Ariel handed Maria a small box; in it the Excalibur processors. Satisfied and fortified by Ariel's proof, she opened it.

"Oh my God, these are the chips everyone's rumoring about," said Maria. "They even look different. I hope Elaine can figure out how to wire them."

"Just do your work. I will deflect those who try to stop you," said Ariel. "Your task is great but your reward greater."

"You promised we would have help."

"And you will, but remember that Satan is attempting to convince even our angels to join him."

"They will refuse, of course."

"Be not sure. Legions followed him when he defied God. His message deceives. Only when he is bound again can we rest."

"He won't deceive me."

"But he will try you and all those with you. You must warn Elaine that this 'Michael' is about. Tell her to shout 'Lucifer' at him. He will understand."

"Will he harm her?"

"Not directly. He will try to convince her, like he tried to convince you."

"He's pretty imposing with his bag of tricks."

"Warn her of that, too. I must leave now."

"When will you return?"

"When you next need me."

9

Sunday Evening

Elaine could wire anything, given the parameters. Getting those details was Maria's job. It was one thing to steal the chip, another to beg the directions for successfully opening it and reading the internal parts; but to physically reverse-engineer a processor and then use that information to run another one without mistake, well that was something else entirely. But Ariel had promised help when needed and Maria felt a confidence beyond her usual self-assuredness.

Maria entered Infinity at 6:15 PM, using her master print to access areas off-limits to most people. She had to sacrifice one of the chips to Destructive Testing. There was no other way. How she wished she could just pay someone off to get the architecture and working voltages of the Excalibur, but there was no time for that.

Larry had encapsulated the chip in an ultra-tamper-resistant module, full of Permissive Action Links. Just getting into the package itself could set off molecular trip wires that would destroy the chip's functions. The proprietary molding compounds Larry used were known to only a few. Fortunately, Dave's references pointed out detection processes for each of these. Maria entered the subsurface photography lab, placed the chip in the analyzer, and turned on the ultraviolet lamp. Photons from the lamp went into the plastic to a depth of a few microns, knocking out electrons from the substance, and producing a secondary image on the screen. That illuminated the fiber-optic lines mixed into the epoxy, each one an alarm that would destruct if severed. She plasma-ashed them off to get to the next layer.

Then she was faced with the sapphire particles mixed in the plastic. Any mechanical grinding would cause these to explode, wasting the chip. She inactivated these by targeted ablation with a pulsed laser. That brought her down to the first shielded metal layer. She couldn't remove this without wiping out the internal voltages, so she left it in place and circumvented it by magnetic field sensing. She was at the chip surface itself and ready for analysis. Now came the proof of her "gating" device. Maria had to time her test currents to coincide at the nanosecond level with the "down-time" pulses of the numerous circuits. One overlap and the chip would go blank. Then a combination of high resolution micro-photography and voltage contrast electron microscopy allowed her to enter the well gates and analyze all the internal chip voltages, essential circuitry, and the ROM, EPROM, and fast EEPROM cells. Maria looked at her watch. The whole analysis had taken 107 minutes. She wondered if she had missed anything.

All that got her was the state of a static chip. She needed Elaine to wire the sucker, get it operating, and read the operating conditions as it functioned. Doing this under "hostile conditions" would take some luck. They would have to ensure they knew the routings of all the essential circuits, even those buried in polysilicon feeder lines, and make sure the smallest cells would function without disruption. It would be white-knuckle time.

She walked back to her office, pulled the copy of her thesis off the shelf, and left the building.

Elaine held open the refrigerator door, the smell of mold in her face. A heap of Little Debbie Swiss Cream Rolls, Moon Pies, Pop Tarts (which she ate untoasted), leftover pizza, and open boxes of assorted chocolates filled the shelves. She slammed it shut, turning her gaze to the counters that rimmed the kitchenette. Cardboard boxes filled with Nachos, Doritos, Wise Potato Chips, and Cheese Balls beckoned. She grabbed a bag of Pork Rinds, tore open the wrapping, and shoveled them in as she walked toward her bench.

Elaine rejected the amenities of life - like a hermit - rarely washing herself, or doing the laundry, or taking out the garbage. But she was worldly enough to accept the convenience of modern pre-packaging; fast food, vitamin pills, use-it-throw-it-away wrapped essentials. If pressed, she would admit that she liked the color of the dried ketchup spots splattered here and there, even on her clothes. Her t-shirts were for wiping off her hands, and old cream from Twinkies coated the fabric. There were Coke bottle rings everywhere; bacteria finished off the remains of the sugar solution in the bottoms.

A stranger would have guessed that the clothes scattered in groups around the room were the remnants of her last few molts, and would have recoiled to watch her drop one pair of jeans, step into the two pools of legs of another, and pull them up as if they had somehow cleaned themselves when she wasn't wearing them. The only clean things in her apartment were her fingernails, bitten to the quick, and her bright eyes. The violet tinted contacts over her corneas were her one concession to vanity. She wanted eyes like that old movie star Liz Taylor.

Elaine rarely left the house, and when she did it was to get take-out. She hated eating in restaurants because the waitresses insisted on talking to her when they took her order. She had no friends, unless you counted her contacts on the Net. No car either. She had quit the graduate program at Pitt when she realized a degree might make her responsible.

She was very happy.

Maria banged on the door. "Elaine, it's me!"

She heard the chain being removed and the deadbolt sliding open.

Maria went to the work area and sat down. She cradled the box in her lap.

"You have them?" Elaine asked.

Maria opened the box, took out the Excaliburs, and laid them on the white surface.

"What the hell? Who designed these?"

"I don't know and it doesn't matter."

"How did you get them?"

Now was the time to explain about Ariel. Maria's description of the angel and what she had said didn't seem to faze the young girl. She handled the chips as Maria spoke, more interested in how they could connect to a board than in what Maria was saying. Except for the end part.

"So I'm to expect a visit from this bad angel Michael? And we're going to save the world?"

"Yes, and maybe Ariel will show herself to you. I have no way of knowing when and where they'll pop up next."

"This is way cool."

"No, it isn't. Don't you want to know about the 5th World and the battle to come?"

"No. You handle that, I'll be busy."

"How far have you gotten with the structure?" asked Elaine.

"I don't think I've missed anything."

"We'll know soon enough."

Maria marveled at Elaine's ability to focus. Maria had tried to do that all her life, but was always dragged back to normalcy by the reality of her life. It made her less of a scientist, and she hated it. Oh, Maria would get the money and the power, but without the Elaines of the world, most of the real work would never get done. Now she had within her grasp the ability to decide the fate of men. No more would people fail, left to their own devices. The perfect insight Ariel had brought her would turn evil into good. Deep inside she knew it was ordained that her life be given this meaning.

"I'll be back in the morning to work with you. That will give you time to define the parameters you'll need to connect these."

Elaine nodded. Since she had ceased to exist in Elaine's world, Maria let herself out and went home.

Elaine picked up the Excalibur and examined the connections. You couldn't plug this one into any existing board and have it fit. It was wider than a P16, thicker too, and the number of pins exceeded 8000. "Should have called it the multi-millipede," she thought.

She clamped small tweezers onto one terminal and held the chip to one side. Then she turned it under a magnifying lens. The structure was beyond practical; it was beautiful, designed by an artist in love with his work, someone who knew the pleasure of a perfect device. She admired the workmanship, the attention to detail, the thoroughness. She'd like to meet the maker.

When she put the processor down, she noted that all of its protrusions touched the pad at once, no patio table wobble. She wondered if it would overheat, like the early Pentiums, but thought "no," not with the attention to detail that was so evident. Enough care showed on the surface to convince her that inside the layout was perfect.

But she had to test it anyway, so she screwed it into a padded microclip-vise, connected micro-leads, and started the protocol. It was like checking and rechecking an ideal flower, looking for a thorn.

When things got busy, Maria cleared the decks. She called her superior at Infinity and told him she wanted the week off.

"You know I need you this week," he said.

"Jack, you need me every week."

"But we want the Fiddler program finished before the New Year. ToyBox is crunching us to deliver on time."

"The hell with ToyBox. I haven't had a day off in two years. I need a week now!"

"Okay, okay. What for? Travel?"

"Jack, it's my business."

"Just this once, Maria. But I need you in early after Christmas."

"Sure. Sounds like a lifetime away," said Maria.

"Odd answer," he thought, but then Maria was strong willed, deserved some time off, and it really was none of his business.

Ariel had passed the test; she got the chips. How she did it was not Maria's concern. Something was in the works; things looked real. Ariel warned Maria not to miss any sleep. She wanted her alert, not fogged with exhaustion.

Maria thought about calling her parents to tell them she wasn't going to the Rainbow Room, but Ariel told her not to make any decisions without talking to her first. And she had promised her father that she would think about it until Monday. So she lay in bed and wondered. Activity was one thing, but having to coordinate others, while, supposedly, the fate of the world hung in the balance, was another. Neither a drinker, nor a smoker, Maria had little to distract her. She turned on the TV. Football games. She wondered which one John was watching. Maybe she should call him to talk about not going to New York, but then, he knew that anyway. She had to get a grip. She was so pumped she couldn't sleep, so she called Cassie.

Cassie picked up the phone after three rings. "M^3? Long time no hear."

"I've been busy."

"Don't try that on me, I know you too well. You want to talk."

And talk they did, about John, Infinity, her parents, all Maria things. As an afterthought Maria asked, "How are things with you?"

Cassie told her, although she knew Maria wasn't listening. Being Maria's release valve was fine with her. They hadn't actually seen one another since California days, and the calls were few, but their friendship served them both well. At least Cassie had a life outside her job.

"You and Walt?" Maria asked when Cassie finished.

"No change. Maybe when he matures we'll work it out."

"I always thought he was more mature than John."

"And I think the reverse."

"Will we ever be happy?" asked Maria.

"Not if we rely on others."

"I suppose, I suppose."

Whether it was the calm Cassie brought or exhaustion, Maria felt tired. She fell asleep in her clothes and was dreaming in minutes.

10

Not Just *Any* Dream

Maria was perched on the Phonak sign above the Renaissance Hotel, with a clear view of the crowd in Times Square. It was less than a minute to midnight on December 21st, and the people were counting off the seconds to the 5th World. The rooftops around her were full of dark figures, some hanging by what appeared to be tails from the balustrades. They weren't rejoicing like the people below.

Ten, 9, 8, 7. The ball was almost to the base of the pole atop the Times Square building. The only time it had ever been used for something other than New Year's Eve. Horns were blaring in the streets.

Three, 2, 1. The ball went out. The crowd started singing, "We are the World, we are the people…" locking arms and swaying with the music.

Then a loud crack filled the air, followed by a rumble like a massive train passing. The building shook; Maria held on. The first shrieks came from below. A large chasm opened on 46th Street. From the vent forms issued, crawling onto the street. The creatures on the other buildings leapt down, gliding on bat wings, and threw themselves at the crowd.

The building continued to shake; cracks appeared on all the streets. Then the Trump building, on Maria's left, collapsed, sending stone and brick down on the people below. Maria looked across at the Times Square building. There was Satan, his enormous thick wings covered the roof, his rat-like body hovered on the rail, his tail wrapped around the flagpole. From his mouth issued tongues of fire; his anus spewed black boiling tar; his breast opened and hordes of demons appeared, raining onto the people below.

Then she saw the screen on the big illuminated NASDAQ Mikohn Vision sign, that before had shown live video of the happy people, start flashing the number "666." Weird music reverberated off the buildings: dissonant strings, drums off beat, horns that grated the ears. The 744,000 lamps on the bright sign then filled the screen with horrifying scenes, as if a mad reporter were filming a world gone wild. A woman was pinned against the ticket office at 47th Street, held off her feet, her legs grasped at each ankle by a demon, being raped by monsters until their huge penises split her in half. In front of The Disney Store, a family was being tortured. First, they were stripped of their clothes, then held in the hands of Ashtaroth, who licked them with her barbed tongue, tearing flesh with each stroke. The children screamed, their parents helpless.

In front of the marquee announcing "Sean Connery in *Father Time*" lay a curled serpent, spitting venom from its mouth, paralyzing its victims. Then it slowly slid its head up their bodies, its tongue hissed as it passed their necks. When it came to each face, it opened its jaws wide and slipped its mouth over the head, leaving an air passage at the sides so the person wouldn't die yet. The victim's head was sucked in first, the serpent undulating its neck so the shoulders and torso could slide in. The petrified prey moved down into the body of the snake. Once a person was past its neck, the snake turned to the next one and sucked it in. Maria could see the snake roll and hump as the people tried to get out. Stomach acid ate at their skin.

Near the statue of Father Duffy, bodies were being thrown in the air, some already dead. Grotesque monsters shat on the effigy of the soldier priest, others coiled around the statue's body in lewd poses. Maria saw the eyes of the statue blink, as if the real priest were imprisoned inside. Arioc, dressed as a nun, mounted the statue and started humping it from the front. Another demon mounted it from behind.

All along the great boulevard of Broadway, men were impaled on the tops of lampposts. Each move they made to free themselves drove the metal in farther, their bound hands useless and bleeding. On some posts the tip had already penetrated through the stomach; on others the point kept plowing upward, piercing as far as the neck. They were not dying. And all of this was being broadcast worldwide.

Down Broadway from the north came The Rider of the Second Seal on a red horse, wielding a great sword, slaying people as he came forth. His great blade whooshed in the air, decapitating scores of people with one swipe. Human heads flew in the air and bounced off the sides of buildings. Some rolled in among the crowd, eyes still open. When the Rider reached 50th Street he reined in his horse, the giant hooves disemboweling people.

He cried out, "Where is your God now?"

From the south, up Seventh Avenue, came a Pale Figure on a Pale Horse, Death, The Rider of the Fourth Seal. The legions of Hell followed him, scurrying into the side streets, from which issued wails and screams never heard before. But Death rode on to the middle of the square in front of the Marriott Hotel, where he reigned in his mount, prancing on its hind legs, and looked at Maria with his black eyes, a hideous smile on his death face.

"Know now that you are doomed," he spat. "I will kill you last so you can witness what you wrought."

Death turned in his saddle and blew a blast of frigid air over the people. Faces cracked open, limbs shattered, bodies burst, sending pieces to the ground. Then he opened his arms wide and gathered hundreds of people to his side. They froze on contact and fell in broken piles at the hooves of his mount. Hideous laughter gushed out of his mouth, so loud it shattered windows for blocks around.

Maria turned away from the scene before her and looked east. Above Saint Patrick's Cathedral she saw an opening in the sky and a vision like the Hell Ariel had shown her. Wretched souls, chained in long rows, were being led from the ground into the hole by Baalim. Those who stumbled were pierced by forks, wielded by devils, and held high for the others to see.

The world watched in horror, then despair entered every heart. Those who tried could not turn off their TVs, others feared turning off the horror as if by viewing it they could remain untouched. Some held to the scene by rapture, others by fear. Chaos began.

Brimstone came out of the vents in the street and spread over the people like lava. It slid up the sides of stores, even to where people were perched on the tops of cars. On contact, it melted flesh and drew the bodies down into a fiery death. The stench was overwhelming.

Screams from people being eaten filled the air. A banker was stretched against a building, his face held up by a clawed hand. A funnel was jammed in his mouth and Mammon poured molten gold into its opening. Smoke from his burning throat pulsed in the air.

Women and men who had lusted were violated in every orifice. A handsome man was being carried down the street, a pole through his anus, a demon cock in his mouth, his penis was being sucked by a razor-filled mouth. A beautiful woman, dressed to the nines, was being reamed by a spiked cone in her vagina, her breasts seared by a bra full of hot coals, her face imprisoned in a rack of knives. Each movement of her head brought deep cuts. Belial, the most lewd, taunted her.

Nisroc tied the unforgiving to racks and slowly stretched them, cracking their bones. The more they cried for help, the more they suffered.

Maria looked around for help but there was none. Every face she encountered, whether of man or demon, ignored her.

"Please!" she shouted. "Stop - stop!"

Her next cry startled her. She was awake; sweat rolled down her face, she bit the pillow and tried to get a hold of herself.

11

Monday Morning
December 17th

Maria lay in bed and stared at the ceiling, exhausted from her nightmare. She willed herself to focus on her work. The first part seemed clear. She and Elaine needed to have the circuits finished for the Wednesday evening test run. Then what?

Ariel appeared at the foot of the bed, floating above the floor so Maria could see her while still supine.

"We will be ready in time," said Maria, surprising herself in her certainty. "What happens after that?"

"Tell your parents you will go with them to New York."

"What? I don't have time for them. They'll be in my way."

"The trip will give you reason to be there; that will camouflage your real intent."

"Which is what?"

"The Demon and his horde will use communication as a weapon," she began, and then explained how Satan would proceed. He had minions all over the world, ready to seize TV-transmitting stations. Through these he would speak to most of the world's people, frightening them with scenes of destruction and descriptions of his victory over the forces of good. Those not directly harmed by his legions would still witness the torture of their brethren, and fall into despair. It dovetailed with the dream.

By dominating the airwaves and super-saturating men's minds with images of their own destruction, Satan would obliterate the good implanted by their religions. He would erase the images of hope and love. Then the evil embedded in man by original sin, which he had learned to control with great effort, would be released.

Despair, the greatest sin, would spread among all, culminating in suicides and mass panic. Once they realized there was no hope, people would stop work, stop play, stop prayer. Neighbor would turn against neighbor, husband against wife; brothers and sisters would kill one another. Souls would be damned.

Thinking there was no salvation, each man and woman would become an island of greed, trying to survive the engulfing wickedness. For some, the end would be quick, but others would live for years, hiding from daylight, hunting their kind, fighting over scraps.

The debasement of humankind would signify the triumph of darkness over the soul of man. God would turn His face away.

Ariel moved near the dresser and elaborated the plan to prevent all this. New York was the world center of communications and the staging ground for the heralding of the 5th World. The computer Maria would build would be installed at the base of the tower atop the Times Square building. It would be activated by contact with the New Age lighted ball when it descended at the stroke of midnight. At that very moment, Maria's device would black out the Devil's attempt at transmission, and allow Ariel and the good angels to show this world the peace of the next World.

"The timing is important," said Ariel.

"But my parents will expect me to be with them when the world turns."

"You will, until the very last. Do not worry about their reaction."

"My God, that probably means John will come also."

"You will handle that."

"Why do you have such confidence in me?"

"You have help."

Ariel left, and Maria got up and dressed. She was trying to control her anxiety and proceed at a fast but steady pace. She knew she worked best that way. Fewer mistakes.

Maria stopped at an IHOP for breakfast. Forget diet food; she wanted something solid to see her through the day. On the way, she bought two honey buns and a quart of orange juice for Elaine. She concentrated on her driving, which only seemed to make it more difficult. She was relieved when she pulled onto Elaine's street. Elaine was at the door on first knock.

"Let's start," she said. "I can wire these suckers."

"You have the P20s and the motherboard?"

"Yep. All I need is the sequence of contacts and the drain for each chip. How much redundancy are we planning?"

"None."

"None? Are you sure?"

"This is like a space mission. It either works for the test and one use or it doesn't."

"My jeans are getting warm."

Maria didn't waste time describing what she'd brought; she just laid it out.

"A Norvell microtip soldering probe? How chic, boss."

"Ten times as good as that nail you're using," said Maria.

Then there was the miniwire, the Josephson junctions, the monoatomic spray, the teflon bridges, the Slinky.

"A Slinky?"

"It calms me down," said Maria.

"Don't go wild on me."

Elaine was munching on a honey bun directly over the circuit board.

"I wish you wouldn't do that."

"Watch how I eat. I've got a method that eliminates crumbs."

Elaine bit into the bun with a sucking sound, then rotated it up and extended her tongue. When the bite was over she licked the inside to stick any crumbs to the surface before she bit again. Then she took the baby drinking cup she had modified by closing all the suck holes except one. She sucked fluid up so she wouldn't have to hold the cup upside down and risk a spill. Her Daffy Duck bib with the crumb catcher was a backup.

Elaine swung the body of her Zeiss 125X Stereo Microscope out and over the pristine board. She inserted the Norvell tip into the front of her soldering iron and tightened the boom clamp. Once the open wires came into view, she punched the coordinates into the drive computer to establish laser positioning. Her hands worked the micromanipulators that dampened her movements by a factor of 100. If Maria's angel appeared, Elaine could put it on the head of a pin.

Maria worked on the design. Her portable PowerPlatform showed the configuration on a blue gray background: green lines for finished circuits, red for those Maria was testing for compatibility, flashing yellow for circuit dumps. She worked in the changes with the stroke of a few keys, the circuit getting smaller as she whittled at the connections she could eliminate.

The numbers were another problem. Maria was sure she could arrange them in sets small enough to leave space for run-overs. She was surprised herself at how sophisticated the program she had designed in graduate school still was. Of course, Ariel would have known that.

She wondered if the angels were working with her back then, preparing her for this day.

"There should be an M4 lead on the left."

"I see it," said Elaine.

"Connect that to the fifth terminal point above bus 8."

And so it went as the two women worked.

A small wisp of vaporized Bakelite and solder rose above the micro-manipulators to Elaine's fingers. The microscope, held in its cantilevered holder, prevented most of the smoke from reaching into her nose and eyes. It didn't matter; Elaine loved the smell.

Neither moved for the next four hours. They acted as one unit: Maria the brain, Elaine the hands. Occasionally, Elaine would correct one of Maria's orders, but the Excalibur design melded in with most of what Maria needed done.

Elaine was working in the fourth quadrant now. The micro-tip of her iron touched the last junction, fused it together, and completed the circuit. She sat back, moved the scope out of the way, and admired her work.

The two Excalibur chips were wired in parallel, enabling them to perform separate functions, relieving each from the routine of keeping the program in operating mode. That work was handled by the P20 chips Elaine had scavenged from her own computers. Altogether, the new hardware had computing power beyond belief and tuned to one purpose only. There was nothing like it in the world.

Elaine and Maria marveled at what they had made.

"They got rid of the backwards compatibility redundancy," said Maria. "That freed up all the chip's power for my program."

"I never expected to see a 10,000 mega-hertz chip this soon," said Elaine. "And it doesn't even heat up much."

"Remember, silicon is just sand and the new germanium-arsenide architecture eliminates energy transfer. We're right on the verge of sub-atomic limits."

The completed motherboard was only 4 inches by 2 inches. Elaine would run a drop-test later. That would allow her to read the algorithm embedded in the microcode. But she was at a loss to write a ratcheting sequence to connect the terminals. Even Maria couldn't help her with that. If she could solve that, she could build the rest of the box by tomorrow. Maria would begin de-bugging runs Wednesday. Then it was on to the test. No outside opinions, no exhaustive in-house trials, no sharing the blame. No, this was cottage stuff, wire-fire-don't-make-me-a-liar.

"Lunch?" asked Maria.

"Not interested. I'll eat later."

There was a knock on the door. Elaine looked nervous. "No one visits me."

Maria opened the door, keeping the chain on.

"Delivery boy," he said, holding up the bags from a Chinese restaurant.

Maria let him in.

"All paid for," he said. Maria tipped him.

Maria cleared a spot on the large table that served as Elaine's desk. She took out the cardboard cartons and arranged them in a row. Paper plates, plastic forks, napkins, soy sauce, fortune cookies - it was all there.

"How did they know I like Moo Goo Gai Pan?" Maria asked.

"And me Sweet and Sour Pork?" Elaine chirped. "I haven't even met them."

"Yes, you have," said Ariel.

Elaine would have screamed if she weren't so scared. As it was, she spewed her food out onto the table.

"I'd better introduce you. Elaine, this is Ariel."

"We have met before," Ariel said.

"No, we haven't."

"Remember the day you fell through the ice when you were skating alone?"

"That was years ago."

"Moments to me," said Ariel.

"My father saved me."

"He found you on the ice after I pulled you out of the frozen water."

"That was you? Dad asked me how I got out. They said I must have done it unconsciously and then blanked out."

"As good a story as any. We do not seek credit, Elaine. In fact, we shun it."

"I thought you were my guardian angel," said Maria.

"I work with those whose life lines interact."

"Why are you here now?"

"To insure that Elaine knows the truth. Her support is vital to your work."

"Other than the box, I don't know sh.... anything."

"Listen to Maria, and know that you will succeed. God is with you both."

"Can I call on you if I need help?" said Elaine.

"No, but I will come when my intervention is most important."

"Like with the food?"

Ariel smiled, first at Elaine, then at Maria. Then she levitated above the workbench, looked down, and smiled again. Elaine glanced at Maria. By the time she glanced back, Ariel was gone.

"Jesus, you have weird friends."

"I think we should eliminate the profanity just to be on the safe side," said Maria. "I don't understand this much more than you do now. Let's just do our part and hope for the best."

"We're working for God?"

Maria nodded.

Elaine let out a war whoop. "God...I mean, yes, I'm hungry!" she said.

When they finished, they broke open the cookies. They both got the same fortune: "You shall know the truth and the truth shall make you free."

Elaine turned hers over and saw the six lucky number series. She recognized it as a ratcheting sequence.

12

Monday, Noon

The last time she had called the number it was to argue over who got the Porsche. But project came before pride and she was dialing it once more.

"Hello," said John.

"John, this is Maria..."

"Maria, I know your voice."

"Sure, I'm calling about New York."

"I'm not going either."

"I know that's what you said, but...I mean, I wonder if I could change your mind?"

"No. But why?"

"Well, it's my parents. Dad has wanted this for years."

"Since when have you put their concerns first?"

"John, please, let's not argue. I just called to tell you that I'm saying yes to them. I wanted you to know."

"Before I turn them down?"

"Could I ask you to say yes?"

"*Could* I ask you? Maria, what do you really want?"

She looked in the mirror above the phone, set her teeth, and said, "I'd like you to come."

"For yourself or your parents?"

"For me."

"Maria, I can't read you at all. Saturday you were a cold fish, now this. I'm building another life here..."

"Please say 'yes' this one time and I won't ask again."

John knew what his answer would be, but he paused anyway.

"All right."

"Good, I'll call them now."

"No, you call for yourself. I'll call tomorrow for me."

"Thank you," she said and hung up, red with embarrassment. He was such a jerk.

The next call was easier. Sal picked up the phone, nestled between two photos of Maria as a young girl.

"Dad? I can make it for the party in New York."

"Really?" Looking across the room at Rosa, he whispered, "She's coming."

Then, to Maria, "Let me get the tickets so I can tell you the times."

Rosa turned toward the bay window. Except for their own wedding picture, the studio portrait of Maria and John dominated the sill. On the end table was a smaller photo of them dancing at the University Ball in the Cathedral of Learning at Pitt, Maria in a green taffeta dress.

"They were such a perfect couple," she said.

Maria didn't mind using John and her parents. Ariel's work transcended that, and they could be told later. The angels could plan things, but they needed Maria to act them out. Even John was always preaching to her about the power of images. Well, controlling how the world would view the turning of the millennium was beyond any artist, beyond any system, until Maria and Elaine finished The Savior.

And using the Times Square event was brilliant. Everyone, even the stay-at-homes, was primed to watch that. Groups from all over the world were sending delegations. Mayan shamans and dancers were already there practicing for the cameras. The world's eye would be turned to TV, New York TV, and that would be controlled by Maria.

The secretary to the head of the National Computer Security Center of the National Security Agency (NSA) in Fort Meade, Maryland, looked up at the woman with the press pass clipped to her blouse, the firm breast holding the badge horizontal.

"I have no appointment scheduled for you," she said.

"Oh, I know. I am doing a story for *Newsweek*, and I want to see the director."

"I doubt if Mr. Hinkel has time..."

Just then, Hinkel opened his office door, said something to the secretary, then noticed Miranda.

"Since when have we been issuing press passes?" he asked.

She repeated her request.

"I didn't tell her you'd see her, Mr. Hinkel..."

"That's okay, Barbara." He motioned to the woman to follow him.

Miranda, a nanocassette video recorder hidden on her left arm, followed Hinkel into his office. She explained her mission in more detail.

"Who told you I would allow you to see that room?"

"No one. I just thought our readers would like an insider's description."

"No photographs and I get to read the copy before it's printed."

"Of course."

"Remember what NSA really stands for: 'Never Say Anything,'" said Hinkel.

Miranda laughed. Then they walked down the hall and entered a large room, lit in a soft blue light.

"This is where we access all communication codes," said Hinkel. "Everything is encrypted."

"Can a foreign power steal our codes?" she asked.

"Not anymore. We've plugged all the shadow leaks..."

"Shadow leaks?"

"Our signals are partly traceable, like my shadow follows my size and shape. But you couldn't make an accurate picture of my face from it."

"Do you try to steal other countries' codes?"

"Well, yes. It's a constant battle, even among allies."

Hinkel had no idea why he was opening up to this girl. Maybe it was the drop-dead gorgeous, the legs that went all the way up. He'd be interesting but careful.

"How do you do that?" she asked.

"We try programs that run the encryption process backwards, so we see the passwords that lead to the vaults."

"Vaults?"

"Not a real vault, but a term for where the codes are locked away."

"I'll bet you've broken quite a few?"

"Well, not just me. I have help," he bragged.

"What do the codes look like?"

"You wouldn't understand them; they're all in an arcane computer lingo."

"Could a good hacker decipher them?"

"Almost impossible, unless he could program a backwards driver. You could translate rongo-rongo before you could read these."

"So, you're not at risk showing them to me?" she said, putting her hand on his arm and running her tongue over her red lips.

"Not really," said the shaking man.

He looked around. No one was watching, so he called up a screen labeled "Sherlock." He scrolled the 19 frames quickly, displaying 197 country codes.

Miranda kept pointing at the screen, the video recorder wiring away, the 2 mm nano-camera, phase-locked in TV mode to remove flicker, shooting everything.

"We're not sure that some haven't been changed, but we check the major countries every day. We change ours dozens of times a month, using a random number generator."

"This is so fascinating. My readers will love it," she said.

"Let me walk you back to security."

"Thanks, but I know the way and I have to visit the ladies' room."

God - I'd love to follow you in there, Hinkel thought. He said, "Well, it's been nice talking to you," coughed once, "come again."

"Start again, Larry," said Bill Traynor. "This is Captain Lucas from downtown."

The story gushed out, a plea for forgiveness in every word. Larry ended with, "She's a demon. She enticed me to give her chips, and then she left."

"How do you know she's a demon?" asked Lucas.

"Michael told me so; he's an angel."

"I see. Thank you, Larry. Please stay handy; we might need you again."

Larry got up and went back to the lab.

"You weren't kidding," said Lucas. "He's popped a head gasket."

"Yeah, but there are still three Excalibur chips missing. We're talking over $190 million in research and development costs down the chute if they're in the wrong hands. Have you been able to trace the girl?"

"She's vanished, if she ever existed. We've contacted all your competitors to alert them of the penalties for this type of theft. We've started reading his emails from the last five years. Could take a while."

Then they discussed the other possibilities: foreign firms, foreign militaries, crazy hackers, a madman. And looming over them all was Intel; the Excalibur would bite heavily into their lion's share of the market.

"He's under constant surveillance," said Lucas.

"Shouldn't you just lock him up?"

"No, he might lead us somewhere."

"Unless he stole them himself."

Traynor swiveled his chair and looked out over the Allegheny River.

"We make things so small you could slip a few in your mouth and walk away."

"But you have detection devices at all exits," said Lucas.

"Yeah. How did she or 'Michael' avoid those?"

Lucas stopped again at security. He asked to see the surveillance systems once more.

"Looks tight to me."

"We could detect a mosquito carrying a virus, if it tried to leave without going through a check point."

"And no one saw anyone come in near that time?"

"We have some lab rats that work on Sunday - Larry is one of them - but you've talked to all of them already."

"How about janitors, outside repair men, the telephone company?"

"All accounted for by our detection devices."

"Are you absolutely sure?"

"You know what happens if someone tries to leave with something we've tagged?"

"You bag 'em."

"Not just that. Tire claws come up on all roads, laser beams intersect over the whole site, each capable of downing anything that flies, searchlights make the place look like Alcatraz, guard dogs are released, the sound generators don't shut off until we deactivate them, and all perimeters are sealed."

Lucas searched to see if there was any hole a pro could slip through. It seemed impossible.

"Okay, but run those tapes again and look harder for anything unusual."

Larry was sitting in the office just off his lab, waiting for the next interrogator. This one knocked on the open door. He didn't look like a cop.

"Larry, I'm Claude Devon, from the VA Hospital, Leech Farm. I'm a psychiatrist, but don't be alarmed. I don't think everybody's crazy."

"Maybe I am," said Larry.

"We'll see about that."

Devon ran a series of standard tests on him. He also allowed Larry to go on about what he thought had happened. It took almost 90 minutes.

"You don't fit the patterns. I think you interacted with someone. If you can give me some physical evidence that Miranda exists we may be able to get the police to do their job and find her."

Larry wondered what he could use. Miranda had ways of keeping his mind on her. She had stuffed her lace panties in his hand after sex yesterday. He opened a drawer in his desk and pulled them out.

"We'll have them fingerprinted," said Devon. "Maybe she has a record. Anything else you can think of?"

They discussed her car, the things she touched in his apartment, whether she had left a strand of hair somewhere.

"The police have dusted your place. No fingerprints except your own."

"See, she's not human. Maybe she doesn't leave fingerprints."

"Larry, I need your help. There are enough clues in the literature, and many more by those afraid to publish, that these things really happen. I assume you've bathed since you had sex with her on the desk?"

Somewhat ashamed, Larry replied, "Not really. I've been too busy, with the cops and all."

"Good. Let's go downstairs to the clinical lab and see what she left on you."

Ordinarily, Larry would have walked out when the doctor made his request. But he knew this was important, that Miranda was up to something cosmic, something that had to be stopped. She had used him! He changed into the thin gown and sat on the examining table.

"Would you prefer a nurse do this?"

"No, no nurse."

The doctor raised the robe, took a small blade and carefully scraped the congealed mucus and skin off Larry's penis.

"Any oral or anal sex?" asked the doctor.

"No."

Back upstairs, Lucas looked across at Larry. "We can handle the foreign stuff, and the true nut cases, but we need you to help with the hackers. Can you tell us the best ones?"

Larry knew the famous ones, but they were usually leap-frogged quickly by newcomers. What he tried to do when compiling his list was to limit it to the few who could install a new chip without the blueprints. That narrowed it down to 17.

"But each of those 17 may know a few others," said Larry. "So you may have as many as a hundred out there."

"Large, but manageable," said Lucas.

"Can I go home now?"

"Yes, but we want an agent with you. He'll be very unobtrusive, but he will listen in on any calls and be right there if you need him."

"Do you think I'm in any danger?"

"If your story is true, you may well be," said Lucas, unconvinced.

Lucas placed a call to Washington. He hated working with the Feds, but knew he might be in over his head. They listened to his careful phrasing of what Larry had told him.

"You don't believe this alien stuff, do you?" they asked.

"Of course not, but I think this may lead us out of Pennsylvania so we want you in."

A local cop asking for the Feds to come in? Ha!

"You'll hear from us in the morning."

"Pricks," hissed Lucas and hung up.

13

Monday Night

The last three days left Maria exhausted. She slid between the covers, popped a melatonin, put the TV on "timer," and slipped into sleep. As she moved down the levels of consciousness, she became aware of a familiar scene. She was back in Times Square, the ball had descended, and the carnage from last night's dream was displayed below her. Then a pulsing light drew her attention to the giant NASDAQ screen on the Times Square Building. It was broadcasting destruction from around the world. Everyone still alive stared at it.

It was early morning, December 22nd, 2012, in Oxford, and the Archbishop of Canterbury, visiting Christ Church, was torn from bed, stripped, manacled in a cage, and held aloft by four devils as they marched up High Street, making him watch the slaughter pouring into the road. Students were mauled in front of the chapels, their entrails hung like bunting over the stone walls. Tutors screamed when tossed into pits filled with vipers. The stench made the Archbishop vomit.

The people of Rome awoke to find their televisions on, blaring music that made their ears bleed; on the screen, a horrible image of the Pope being dragged up a hill where a cross was rammed into the ground upside down. The prelate struggled; his robes were torn off. His mitre was nailed to his head by gnomes, each beat of the hammer sending blood into the air. His rosary was seared into his chest and his mouth was clamped open. Four devils lifted him onto the cross, feet at the top, head down. Huge spikes were driven into his ankles and wrists, each blow resounding into people's homes. The naked pontiff hung there, his torn flesh flapping in the raging wind, blood rushing to his head. Judas pierced his side with a lance and purple blood gushed out. Worms and rats entered the wretched man's mouth. Demons danced around the scene, and above his feet a sign proclaimed, "Peter, the Rock of the Church."

The enormous crowds in Cairo stared in horror as each of the millions of blocks of the great pyramids vaulted into the air then fell onto the screaming crowds. The mummy of Ramses II appeared in the air then exploded into ash. Akhenaten, he of the One-True-God, was shown weeping as his beloved wife Nefertiti was raped.

In the courtyard of the great mosque in Mecca, the faithful pilgrims watched in horror as the wide belt encircling the holy carpet began to unwind. A mocking voice, imitating an Imam, read aloud the texts from the Koran inscribed in gold wire on the belt. Then the black rug fell, revealing the Kaaba, its cube-like structure housing the sacred stones. Yemeni, the southern stone, was fractured into millions of pieces, each hurled at a believer. Then the Black Stone rose from the temple, high into the air. Another voice, coming from the stone and mimicking a Muezzin, said, "Where are the great prophets now? Abraham, Moses, Jesus, Mohammed? They have deserted you! You have come here to fulfill the Fifth Pillar of your faith. You will die here, your journey wasted." Then the stone melted into a flat disk, covering the sky and blotting out the sun. An earthquake shook the desert and the temple crumbled.

Further north, the same earthquake sliced across the Temple Mount, leveling the Dome of the Rock. The beautiful hemispherical roof collapsed, the holy chain that led to heaven falling on the rock below. A vision of Abraham appeared, weeping over the body of the son he had just slain. Mohammed fell from the sky, still mounted on his horse, and landed atop the stone the world held sacred. As the earth rent open, layers of previous temples were uncovered. Devils jumped into the cracks, down as far as the Temple of Solomon, below the marble floor, and into the Holy of Holies. There sat the great Ark of the Covenant, undisturbed for thousands of years. They tore off the lid, reached inside, and pulled out the stone tablets that bore the commandments of God. Satan laughed, "You followed these stern orders, yet you received no salvation. Your God is not God!"

The remnants of the Ethiopian Jews, assembled in Axum, watched their Ark Chapel catch fire, then melt, as if it were butter. The Guardian, he who tended that Ark, burned with the building, his filthy screams rending the air as if from a man possessed. A figure, more demon than human, rose from the ashes and shouted, "No power can slay me, not your God, not any God."

At noon in Bombay, people were being fed to Shiva, the destroyer of worlds. Instead of dancing bells, his ankles were ringed with knives; in his hands he held fire. Each time his foot hit the earth, thousands of Hindus were crushed. Elephants, camels, sacred cows roamed the streets, goring and trampling all in their way. The port turned red from the blood of millions.

All over Kyoto, the great Buddha statues cracked and fell, killing the faithful. The late afternoon sun glinted off scenes of dragons devouring the living. The members of the Diet were imprisoned in a clear ball, and rolled to the top of Mount Fuji. The mountain quaked, then roared, as the ball slid into the boiling caldera.

The first Hawaiian to see the wave that blotted out the waning sun, thought that a vertical black storm cloud was coming from the west. When the mass of water hit the island, docks bent back and upward, buildings buckled and were swept away, and the people were devoured by sea monsters.

In Los Angeles, when the clock struck nine, insects appeared. Not the locusts of biblical times, but enormous bugs, from movies of the fifties. They crawled all over the Hollywood sign and then descended into the valley and along Vine Street. Giant ants pinched people in half, spiders the size of office buildings held their prey down while they sucked out their insides. Crabs, wider than football fields, came up from the beaches and clamped their claws on hundreds with one swipe.

The faithful gathered at Tikal felt the tremors first, then the howler monkeys screamed and jaguars raced into the plaza. Mad toucans, their rigid beaks red with blood, punctured those who tried to run. Then the temples shook and the stones rained onto the crowd. Quetzalquatel tried to help his worshipers, but he was vaporized into the air by a lightning bolt. The One Son saw his heart ripped from his body and thrown at the screaming people. Mayan Lords came up from the underworld, led by Pacal, only to be sacrificed on the very altar slabs they had used to offer the blood-rite to their Gods. The resin-covered humans from the 3rd World poured out from holes in the ground and set upon the survivors. Each fiend wrapped one human inside its sticky black skin. Then all of them began a hideous mocking chant that bellowed their curdelled voices into the damp air, the cries pulsing to the beat of a huge drum.

The Times Square screen filled with the image of Satan, so clear he could be seen a mile away in Central Park, speaking to the world. His language translated for every ear.

"Humans, chosen ones of God, see how He has deserted you! Your cries are wasted, your pleadings unheeded. He will not deliver you from the smallest pain; you are mine forever. Look about you; do you see goodness, justice, mercy, charity, any of the supposed virtues? No! They have been replaced by what you harbored in your vile hearts: deceit, anger, envy, hatred. There is no hope, only the certainty of cruel torture; no relief, only perpetual damnation; no reward, only punishment. And it will be so for all eternity. Your free will has left you no choice; your right to choose is gone; your chance to please Him and join Him in the next life, crushed. Look upon my countenance and despair. Mankind is lost!"

In the Square, the meek, captured by Thammuz, were tied to poles and made to eat the droppings of the vile animals that scurried about. But the demons reserved their worst tortures for the righteous. Gnomes, their twisted features mocking the horrors to come, ran among the throngs, marking the foreheads of those who had never sinned. These were herded to the center of the Square, onto a platform made from the very stones of Hell. Satan himself glided down from his height and ordered his minions to split the holy into four groups.

He cast his malevolent stare at a female in the first group.

"Bring that one to me," he rasped.

The woman's husband tried to shelter his wife, but was thrown off the stage with the shout, "You don't belong here, adulterer."

The Devil looked at the frightened woman and spoke, "You have no sin but that of Adam, My sin. Did you think that would save you? Have you the pride of the blessed? Did you not know that by setting yourself as an example you would be made an example?"

With that the Archfiend began to toy with the woman, rolling her across the stage.

"You've never known the joy of sin. Let me show you its power."

The woman's arms reached out, against her will, and clasped herself to Satan's body. Her legs wrapped around his trunk, pulling him close and causing her to hump up and down on his penis. She screamed for relief, shouting foul curses in the air. Then a red and white liquid issued from her mouth and her body was consumed in flames.

Satan ordered the second group to be brought forward.

Almaged and her helpers began the cruel tortures. They set upon each person with unspeakable wrath, as if virtue had injured them the most. They were torn, tormented, eaten, spat out and eaten again, in a continuous display of horror.

"Yours will be the torture of the 5th World. My minions will keep you alert, able to feel pain, for 50 generations, and then you will be cast into the pits," said Lucifer.

The third group was handed terrible instruments and made to wield them against those in the second. They did this without the desire to hurt, but hurt they did, causing more pain than even the demons. They knew they were doing the Devil's work, but they could not stop.

Finally, the last group was prepared. They were arranged in rings, like cut-out dolls, attached to one another by flesh. The rings were lifted vertically and the whole rolled about the stage.

Every video terminal in the world proclaimed the victory of Satan, who played with the human rings with his left hand, then turned to the camera and said, "You will be displayed for all to see, forever. The damned will despise you for not being in the pit. The virtuous will hate your escape from suffering. But you will know true despair, for you will never be part of either world. When Judgment Day comes, if it comes, you will be the detested ones, shunned by God, shunned by the lost, suspended in space for eternity."

Then he began to ridicule God, shouting, "You made them in Your image, and in Your image they will be tormented."

Time appeared to stop; the Devil turned his glare toward Maria. She felt herself being lifted off her perch and transported, as if on a beam of light, to the stage on which Lucifer stood. A breeze blew her hair back, then quickened and blew off her clothes. She was helpless to stop her motion, or even to scream. When she got near the stage she hung suspended in space, within a foot of the Devil's face.

"Well, my dearest, my *instrument*, let me show you my gratitude," he said.

Slowly he slid his hands down over Maria's naked torso, the slime from his fingers leaving tracks on her skin. His breath was putrid; his eyes oozed green pus. The sores on his body pulsed each time he breathed, the pimples opening and closing. Maria almost passed out from the stench. Yet, as horrid as it was, the movement of his hands, now between her legs, began to arouse her.

"Yes, my love, what little virtue you have cannot stop your craving for me."

Maria tried to resist, but felt her body squirming to the motion of his fingers. His lips began to kiss her, first on the cheek, then on the forehead. Her brain was screaming for her to resist but she turned her lips to his and kissed him on the mouth. The heat from his breath ran down her throat and spread along her loins.

"Oh, please stop," she pleaded. "Please stop."

"Mistress of the fallen, your human will so easily bent to mine," he said. "We will stay together forever."

Then, just as Maria gave herself over completely, he stopped.

"I have all eternity for this," he said. "But first, your reward."

Satan motioned with his head for two demons to come forward. They tied Maria's hands to two poles, her legs splayed out, attached to an iron bar. The middle of the bar was placed in a bed of hot embers, the heat transferring along the length of the bar until it seared her ankles.

Lucifer uncurled the fingers on his left hand; his nails glistened in the red light. He placed her left nipple between his thumb and forefinger and rotated the razor sharp nails. Maria screamed.

"We need those off to get a clean hide," he said.

When both nipples were gone he sliced off the nails from her feet and hands. Then he cut around her lips and eyes, her navel, her genitals, her anus, her nostrils and ears.

"And you wanted to be the envy of all," Satan said, as he scalped the top of her head. "Well, you will be the hated one, my cohort."

Maria stood there, hoping she would die or faint, but she hadn't even bled. That was for later.

"Now, see what I have learned," the Fiend said.

Facing her, he started the sharp nail of his index finger cutting the skin at the top of the back of her head. He continued down past her buttocks and finished at the sole of her left foot. Then he did the right. When the cuts were complete, he motioned for the flayers to come forward.

Four skinners worked on Maria, pulling and rolling her skin until the whole came off in one piece. Satan held it aloft for all to see, the perfect hide of a human, unbroken except for the holes where the eyes and other protuberances had been. He handed it to a valkoid in human form, who carefully placed it over her body, assuming the outward appearance of Maria, but glowing with green and brown fire underneath. The valkoid danced a hideous sexual romp, playing with itself, oozing a putrid scum from the holes in its skin.

Maria was still alert, her tissue crackling as the heat from the fires congealed her blood.

"Don't worry, my love, you will grow a new skin, fresh and ready for the next flaying," said the Dark One. "I will keep you as mine forever. Your fault has damned mankind, and they will damn you!"

The crash landed Maria on her side, her cheek bleed from where it sliced against the dresser. Her screams filled the apartment. The phone was ringing and someone was pounding on her door.

14

Who knows what is behind the Altar
Where the Gods congregate
And the cave opens to the UnderWorld?

Who will fashion the next World
And of what elements?
Will people live there?
Other creatures?

Tell us, oh Alalghom Naom, so we may believe!

Tuesday, December 18th

"Just a bad dream, folks," said Maria, holding the door ajar. "Are you sure you're all right? Is someone in there with you?"

"No, no, I'm fine. I just had a nightmare, that's all. I'm sorry I disturbed you."

"You call us if you have any more of those dreams."

Maria closed the door and leaned back against the wall. Things were unraveling.

She called Elaine. "How is it going?"

"I just tried to call you. Everything should be ready about four."

"I'll be over then. Call if you hit any snags."

After breakfast, Maria went over her design and calculations. She couldn't concentrate. She called John. Why? She didn't know. He wasn't home. Neither was Cassie, nor her parents.

And where was Ariel? She turned on the Weather Channel. Thirty-one degrees and light snow. She put on her anorak, gloves, rubber boots, and headed for the car.

Maria hadn't been in a church in years. She wished she could be kinder to her parents when they asked, but she felt like such a hypocrite. Father Boyne came out of the confessional, genuflected at the altar, and started toward the side door. Maria cut him off.

"Father, can I see you for a minute?"

"Of course. Are you a member of St. Joe's?"

"Father, I'm not a member of anything, but I need to talk to you."

Maria followed the priest into the rectory. In the hall she saw one of John's paintings, entitled The Binding of Satan.

Boyne noticed her examining it. "Do you like it? It's by a local artist."

"Frightening."

"Shouldn't be. Satan is being chained in hell, not let out."

They sat in the living room.

Maria told her story. The priest suspected she was delusional, depressed, or at least disturbed. He had heard tales like this before and as much as he wanted to believe some of them, they were always dead ends. But the woman was well dressed, intelligent, and obviously sincere. He teetered between advising a psychiatrist or Father Malik.

"Maria, what you're saying is more than unusual. Have you spoken to a doctor?"

"I don't need a doctor and I don't need the police. I hoped you might understand."

Boyne told her that she was fortunate. The Archdiocese of Pittsburgh had a famous scholar, well versed in the supernatural.

"He's here investigating the Mary sighting in Uniontown."

"Is he an exorcist?"

"No. But he would know a good one."

He called the Bishop's office. "He's expected back at noon. You have an appointment."

The technician pulled her eyes back from the microscope and turned to Devon.

"The mucus had two types of cells in it, other than the sperm. We typed them for male and female, but without a

DNA sample from the girl we can't make a certain match. But we did look at chromosomes."

Devon listened as the technician explained the results. Yes, there were male cells, with their characteristic 22 pairs of chromosomes plus one X and one Y. And other cells had the female pairs with two Xs and no Y.

"But look at this," she said.

The technician held up a photograph of the girl's chromosomes, all neatly paired by cut and patch, placed in descending order from pair one through 22 and then the two Xs. Next to those she had a set from another woman.

"See the difference?"

"Not really," said Devon.

The technician placed her pen tip at pair 6 of the other woman's set. "Note the slight swelling on this branch here; we call that a puff," she said, pointing to the left wing of the closest chromosome. "And see the small abnormality here," she pointed at the tip of another branch, "where it broke off and fused back on again. Almost all people have some of these differences on a few of their chromosomes. They come from eons of small changes and the mechanical tension brought about by mitosis and meiosis, as parents pass on their genetics to their offspring."

"So?" said Devon.

"There's more. The ends of chromosomes are capped by telomeres. Think of DNA as being a shoelace, the telomere is the plastic tip at the end. It prevents the lace from fraying and, in chromosomes, keeps the ends from sticking to each other and forming rings. We know that telomeres are always changing; they lengthen and shorten repeatedly, due to aging and stress, adding to the variation we would expect. They usually shorten as a cell gets near the end of its maximum number of divisions, so sometimes we can even estimate the age of a person by the telomere length."

"I'm still with you."

"So variation is the norm, you see."

"Okay."

"Well, since everyone has these types of abnormalities, it would be very difficult to cull out one individual from another without a court-ordered reference sample or a complete DNA scan, but look at the girl's set I just showed you."

Devon looked, then shrugged his shoulders.

"They're perfect," said the technician. "I've never seen a perfect set before. This is one odd bird."

Father Malik didn't look like a scholar or even a priest. He was wearing a lumberjack shirt, sporting a full beard, a bulbous nose, and a set of lucid eyes, more suggestive of merriment than demonology. His field was not exorcism; that was a mere sideline. He was an archeonumerist, trained to predict the cosmic cycles. An Egyptian, raised as a Coptic in the Church of Mary where the Holy Family had lived during their flight to Egypt, he was deeply versed in the ancient pyramidic codes, and fluent in several languages, including Mayan: he had already booked to stay with the Franciscans on 31st street in NYC for the 5th World events. He knew *The Book of the Dead*, the Mayan *Popol Vuh*, every word in the *Apocalypse*, every stone in the Holy Land, every important Temple in the world. He felt deeply that the turning was at hand but couldn't predict what would happen or what the final outcome would be. He was frustrated.

He asked Maria to sit, lit another Egyptian cigarette, and topped off his drink. She refused offers of both.

"I will ask you simple questions, Maria. Please answer them as truthfully as possible and don't hide anything, no matter how embarrassing, or bizarre, or small you think it is."

Father went down his list: bright lights - no; odd smells - no; offers of money - no; fame - yes; did they just appear - yes; which angel appears to be good - Ariel; what do you dislike about Michael - distant, judgmental; do they perform tricks - yes, I think so; make promises - yes.

"You may have seen something," Father continued. "Why does it disturb you so?"

Maria explained she was a scientist, rational, areligious, not given to flights of fancy. But the foretelling of the battle about to be waged at the turning from the 4th to the 5th World scared her.

Malik bent forward. "What have they told you of the turning?"

"Not much, Father. They give it to me in pieces, quotes from the Apocalypse, tales of times past, horrible dreams, threats."

Malik sat back. This woman had experienced something. He sensed she might lead him to a deeper understanding of the turning. He knew the reports, the Bible, the prophecies. What puzzled him were her angels. They weren't the ethereal beings of Aquinas, nor the demigods of Milton. They sounded much like Malik thought they would: serene, calculating, sure. But could Maria really be the chosen one to thwart the Demon's scheme? Hardly.

"So Ariel took you to see Heaven and Hell?"

"Yes."

"And Michael?"

"I'm sure he's responsible for the nightmares."

"But you've only seen him once."

"So far. I'm afraid he'll come back. He seems determined to frighten me."

Malik spoke directly of angels. Yes, some were good, and some were bad. The highest angels, the Seraphim, Powers, Thrones, made up the bulk of the followers of Satan and fought by his side in the celestial wars. Some scholars thought Satan was the chief angel before the fall, and, yes, he rules from Hell, until the day he is released.

"Again, some students of scriptures say that's every cycle, while others say we have no way of knowing what the quote from Apocalypse means."

"That's not much help, Father."

"It never is on matters as important as this."

"So you can't help me?"

"I didn't say that. We may be venturing into a realm where neither of us can do much. But I do know one thing - we have to work together."

"That's what I want, help."

Father Malik consoled her, telling the stories of great people who were visited by angels, and, when they left this world, became angels themselves

"The Annunciation by the angel frightened Mary, almost to despair," he said. Malik continued with the story of how Mary lived with the shame of being pregnant, not by her husband, how she leaned on Joseph for help, was there for the Christ Child, watched her only Son as he was crucified for others - many unworthy - but lived to rise triumphantly into Heaven, never knowing death. And, she spent her last years in Turkey, near the place where John wrote the Apocalypse.

He went further, describing how Mohammed communed with angels, using the gifts they brought to become a great prophet, before he vaulted into heaven on his horse, from the very rock upon which Abraham was set to kill Isaac and Jesus gave His sermon. And how Siddhartha cleansed himself of the things of this world, denied the flesh, withstood the temptations of evil, and, with the help of heavenly beings, became the Buddha.

"Father, they were in a different league."

"Who knows what He knows and wants? He said a man must be humble, childlike, to achieve the divine."

"Do you know of the 5th World?" she asked.

"Haven't you read any of the dozens of recent books about this?"

"No, I thought they were all hooey."

Malik frowned. "Most are; not all. Maria, the 5th World may be a mystery, or hokum, but if it's real, we'd better be ready for it. It's what we are all trying to understand." Then he told her.

The Mayan writings had been largely destroyed by the Spanish during The Conquest. What remained, especially the Popol Vuh and the Dresden Codex, gave insights into their cosmology, but, in themselves, were not complete. Scholars made progress, deciphering the glyphs that lined the temples, examining the ruins, finding new artifacts; and, piecing together the Mayan view of the world from their wonderful astronomical accomplishments. The Mayans knew the heavens, had discovered magnetic field lines, knew how the planets wandered in the sky. They also possessed remarkable mathematical skills that led to the construction of world cycles. And with those they were able to understand their legends, their place, mankind's place in the universe. Mayans wove the three earthly regions into one fabric through which all beings could pass, Gods from the Starry Arch of the Sky, humans from the Stony MiddleWorld, demons from the UnderWorld.

Malik showed her how they measured, the simple count, based on the twenty toes and fingers, the katun, the baktun. She showed him the bar on her palm. "5," he said in wonder.

But the Mayans went further, deciphering the sacred numbers 7 and 13, establishing the sacred round (260 days) and, finally, the Long Count, what we call one cycle or one World. The next cycle starts when the sun appears from earth to be at the center of our galaxy at the winter solstice, December 21, of this year. That "First Sun," was the symbol for the "First Son," the Mayan ruler who started this cycle.

Maria told her what Sal had remembered being told of the four Worlds from his boyhood.

"Yes, that's a simple description and really enough for us," said Malik. "Just know that this date is so important that all religions point to it, even though most won't admit that."

Malik went on about the Antichrist and whether he would be part of the new world, as some believed, and whether he was here now or even within all of us. "You know, Maria, Islam believes the Antichrist is a one-eyed man, and some think that One-Eye is here now: the TV screen, the computer. I mean, what controls us more than these things?"

Startled, Maria started to speak, then stopped. He had hit too close to home. How much could she tell this man? Should she hold some back, like Ariel did? Could it wait until they met again? Would Ariel tell her whether or not to tell him everything?

"And you know, the Bible does say that the Anti-Christ will come within a generation from the time when Israel will become whole again and armies will assemble all over the Holy Land."

"Where does it say that?" she asked.

"Forgive me, Maria, but you are a typical Catholic, you don't know your Scriptures. It's all in Ezekiel and Zephaniah."

"Now, Israel became a Jewish state in 1948, and armies are there now. Does that mean the Battle of Armageddon will happen before 2048? Not very long, my dear."

Malik then debunked half of what he had just told her. After all, the Jews had returned from Babylon in 65 AD and that was supposed to be the new State but nothing happened for the next hundred years to fulfill the prophecies. And the Scriptures also said the Temple must be rebuilt and that hadn't happened yet. And predictions of the end-of-the-world had been around for as long as religion. Of course, one would be right someday, but when? And were the Scriptures meant to be read as predictions? And were men supposed to be able to calculate these things? Who knew? Why, some even went as far as to add the dates the Virgin of Guadalupe had visited Juan, December 9th and 12th to get 21, the day of the turning! And then they took the time of the winter solstice that will occur that day in 2012 at 11:11 AM and totaled those to 22, the first day of the New World. And the Codex said the 4th World would be destroyed by water. How likely was that?

"I'm not mocking the faithful, Maria. It's just that there's a lot of chaff out there."

"And let's not forget Matthew 24:36, in which Jesus proclaims, "No one knows about that day or hour, not even the angels in Heaven, nor the Son, but only the Father."

Then he went to the bookshelf and returned with two volumes.

"Read these to learn more about the time that's coming," he said. "It's too important not to be ready, just in case. You need to know as much as you can in order to make the correct decision. I am only a phone call away if you need help. How about we meet again tomorrow afternoon?"

"Good for me, Father. It's a comfort to know you don't think I'm crazy."

"We're all crazy, Maria. Belief itself is irrational. But without it we would all go truly mad."

"Thank you, Father," she said, rising to leave. "I wish I were more prepared."

"It's not something you can practice for," he said, and led her to the door.

Then he sat down and wondered.

15

Tuesday Afternoon

When Maria left, Malik called Rome. It was already night there and he had to summon his mentor from evening prayer. He got the authority he asked for, complete freedom to drop his current investigation for a few days and check out the woman's improbable story. Then he went over to the chapel and prayed. He asked God to tell him if Maria was deceiving him; a faker.

"God, in Your wisdom You created us and those not like us. We cannot know their world as they do ours. Our belief is weak, our courage wanes, our understanding only a flicker of theirs. How can we do Your work if they confuse us? Help me to know Your wishes, and help Maria to choose, if she must. We will do Your will if You but show us the way."

He blessed himself and returned to his rooms.

Father Malik knew that demons most hated discovery. They liked to isolate people, cut them off from other humans, leave them no human recourse, no solace. He would need to be present if Michael appeared again. How he could arrange this was unclear.

He called the Bishop and asked for an appointment. Tomorrow morning.

Then he prepared his bag: a vial of Holy Water from the Jordan, a crucifix touched by the Pope, a relic from Padre Pio, dirt from Golgotha, burnt pine needles from the Yucatan, dried lotus from the Orient, ash from the sacred chamber at Karnak. He placed a scapula around his neck, one side showing the Sacred Heart, the other a drawing of Judas hanged. And on the third finger of his left hand he placed a ring, with the Seal of Peter on the front.

He went to the portable bookcase he always kept with him, opened the leather lid, and scanned the 11 titles inside the case. He pulled out Muntzer's *The Battle to Come*, and set it on the table.

The smell of mold rose in the air every time Malik turned a page. He needed to have the book treated or it would disintegrate. He came upon the reproductions from Durer showing the war between the angels; the binding and re-binding of Satan when he was released every cycle; the damned, if the good angels lost; the elect, if they won.

The accompanying text detailed what Muntzer thought of the legends, the traditions, the Scriptures. It wasn't far from what Maria was saying. He also noted what humans must do to aid the forces of good and what they must avoid.

It was clear that mankind could not sit on the sidelines. To prepare for his visit with Maria tomorrow afternoon, he would pray and study through the night.

Devon had trouble convincing the local authorities that they were on to something truly unusual. But they checked with their bio-medical people and confirmed that a perfect set of chromosomes was a one-in-a-hundred-billion chance. Miranda must exist, and may not be truly human or else it was all a clever ruse.

"Then you're buying the demon bullshit?" they asked.

"I'm not saying what she is. She's just not of this world."

"So what does she want with our computer chips?" asked Traynor.

"Who the hell knows, but we'd better find out."

And then there was Larry's other visitation by the angel Michael.

"He claims that fly-boy told him it was a plot," said Traynor.

No one wanted to dismiss it outright this time, but how much of what Larry was saying was real and how much was hallucination?

"He lives in his own kooky little world," said Traynor.

"He wasn't too kooky for you to pay him well to work for you," said Devon.

"You have to understand the computer business. A wife and two kids and a home in the 'burbs is as odd here as Larry and his heavenly hosts."

"Right. So let's assume he's not cloud-dancing and take him at his word. If he's wrong, we get egg on our face. If he's right, we'd better figure this out before it hits somewhere."

Lucas called Washington again.

"That changes things," the contact said. "Put a clear photograph of her chromosome set on the next flight to National."

"Why not scan it in and e-mail it to you?"

"Too blurry. Our techs will need a detailed view."

Lucas called the airport. There was a US Airways flight leaving in 35 minutes. He had it held until his man could arrive.

"Hold onto your seats if they confirm this. You'll hate the arrogant bastard the FBI sends up here. They shit authority."

Devon, Traynor, and Lucas left for the cafeteria. They knew breaks would be few once the ball really got rolling.

"You always slice your donut into segments?" asked Devon.

"So?" replied Lucas. "Don't start analyzing me, Doc. Just because I'm starting to believe in the supernatural doesn't mean the blood's bypassing my head."

"Any news about Larry?" asked Traynor.

"My man says he's just moping around the apartment."

"If he gets whiffly, let me know," said Devon. "How's the list coming?"

"Five down, twelve to go, plus any side contacts. They'll call me if anyone so much as looks upward."

Back in her apartment, Maria started packing for the New York trip. The next few days would be hectic. She decided the black velvet dress was too somber but the green taffeta would suit the mood of hope and bring back memories. It would have to be cleaned and she needed stockings. She'd wear the emerald necklace and earrings John gave her when he'd landed his first ad client. Her dancing shoes needed a brush up (she was surprised how tight they had become), but they would be suitable for her work that night too. For daytime she'd take slacks, a couple of sweaters, boots, and a pair of loafers for lounging. When she got back she would need to do some serious shopping to update her wardrobe.

She was now within 82 hours of the deadline, and she felt more alive than she had ever felt; she knew this was her destiny. She was juggling Elaine, her family, John, her job, her religion, and the angels, all in a mix. Somehow Ariel would make all these conflicting things click, but not before Maria would have to prove that Ariel had chosen well.

"Where is she, where is she?" Maria thought. "Why doesn't she stay with me until it's over?"

After she was partly packed, Maria went over her calculations again. It was odd working on something of such importance without the option of showing it to colleagues. But they wouldn't understand, would they? Suppose she was off by an order of magnitude on some number, or a line was missing from the program, or the test bombed? Would they have time to try again?

"Yes, the test," she said to herself. "Please, God, make it work."

Maria went to the mirror and combed her hair. Ariel had warned her to look and act normal, to avoid suspicion, and to stay alert but calm. She was asking a lot.

But Maria knew she had help. Things were going very well. Everything meshed, everything was proceeding on schedule, everything would work out. Even the thing with her parents and New York. When had Ariel placed that in her father's mind? And what would they all say when she told them later what she had done? Ariel promised that the world would know, would see Maria as an example, would record it for those who had to fight at the end of the next cycle. Jesus God, every cell in her brain was firing!

"Go over to Elaine's and see how things are progressing." Now she was talking aloud to herself. Who cared, she had to talk to someone?

When Maria got to Elaine's, the door was open. Elaine was at her bench, not moving, her microscope light still on, the circuit still in the clip-vise. She wasn't breathing. Maria looked around to see if anyone else was there. Nobody. She tried to determine if the place had been ransacked. Impossible. And why hadn't they taken the circuit board and the Excaliburs?

Maria put down the bag of food she had brought and moved toward the body of the girl. She had never touched a dead person before. Her right hand moved out and grabbed Elaine's shoulder.

"Aaaarrggh!" shouted Elaine, jumping up from her stool.

"It's me!" screamed Maria. "I thought you were dead."

"Dead? Why?"

"Well, the door is open and you weren't moving."

"Can't I get a few blinks? I've been working straight through."

Maria and Elaine hugged in the middle of the room.

"I was worried about you, that's all."

Elaine explained that she had opened the door for some air.

"It's freezing out."

"Air is air. Besides, I was feeling cooped up."

"You? Can we keep it closed until we're finished?"

"Yeah, sure. Hey, look, it's going well."

Maria looked at the board. One of the Excaliburs had been moved from the position she had determined for it. Elaine explained that the chips had been too close, producing magnetic fields that interfered with their functions, so, one had to be moved.

"It goes as the square of the distance," Elaine said. "Sorry, I forgot who I was talking to."

"They must know that. They are probably designed not to be close or to at least be inside a mu-metal cage."

"Yeah, but they work fine now."

Maria started her debugging analysis. She checked each loop of the circuit for conductivity, resistance, capacitance; all sub-circuits were checked for continuity; every feedback loop was measured. Elaine had done her job.

But it was the program that was the challenge. There were over 300,000 unique lines that could pose a problem. Checking each one was impossible within the time frame. Maria split them into groups ranging from 16 to 64 elements. That brought the number of checks down to 5,232. She started in.

Neither woman spoke. The only sounds were of Elaine building the chassis and Maria's hands flying over the keyboard. Every 20 minutes or so one of them would get up, stretch, walk around a bit, and plunge back into the work. It was like they were being watched.

They were.

"Why are you doing the Devil's work?" the masculine voice said.

Maria reeled around, and placed herself between him and Elaine.

"Who the hell is he?" asked Elaine.

"That's where he's from," said Maria.

"You lie, not from arrogance but from ignorance," said Michael.

"Let us alone, Lucifer," Maria said. "Don't frighten my friend."

"Neither of you is important of yourselves. It is his control that makes you so dangerous."

"We won't listen to you."

"Why, Maria? Does the truth scare you so? Can you make a thing from matter, for him to use, without knowing its purpose?"

"I know its purpose, to stop you and your kind."

"My kind? You know little of this world and nothing of the next."

"Enough to know I don't want to share either with you."

"Nor shall you, if you continue."

"How are we to know what's right?" asked Maria.

"You know the rules, but you have covered them with rationalizations."

"Maybe we should listen to him," whispered the quaking Elaine in Maria's ear. "He looks so perfect."

"No more perfect than Ariel." Then to Michael, "If you're so powerful, why don't you strike?"

"I showed you the destruction that will follow your mistake. Need I show more? You must know that your word "video" is from the Latin "I see." Humans have honed that sense beyond all others. You must not let Satan control it."

"Threats and nightmares won't scare me. You'll have to do better than that."

"You must realize that control begets evil and violates free will."

"My choice is my own. No one controls me."

"Yet you wish to control others?"

"No. I'm doing what Ariel says."

"Heed me, not your wicked friend."

"Only if you show me an indisputable sign."

"Our ways are not your ways. You must choose us of your own volition."

"Never will I choose you."

And he was gone again.

Maria helped Elaine sit down, explaining to her about angels and demons.

"Why doesn't Ariel protect you from him?"

"They work in strange ways. I can't figure them out. But he hasn't harmed us yet, just the nightmares," Maria told Elaine.

"Maybe we should ask out of this," said Elaine.

"I don't think that's possible, and I don't want to. But I need your help, Elaine; you can't punt on me now."

They talked some more. Yes, Elaine would still do the work. No, she wasn't scared anymore. She knew how important it was. She wouldn't let Michael scare her.

"He may come to you when I'm not here."

"I think I can handle it," she mumbled

"Pour me some of that *RedBull*," said Maria.

"Starting to drink, boss?"

It took until eleven for Maria to check out the program; her eyes were sore. She would recheck it tomorrow, but it looked solid. Elaine was nodding off too, so Maria put her coat on and bade the girl goodbye.

"It may get worse," said Maria. "But it will be over in 73 hours. Then we'll celebrate like you've never celebrated before."

"I'll take that as a challenge."

They hugged again at the door, the second time ever.

16

Tuesday Evening

Delta flight 691 was bumpy all the way from Reagan Airport in DC to the layover stop in Cincinnati and was even worse during the leg to Pittsburgh. FBI agent Neil King, in seat 15C of the Boeing 737-800, was nauseas with fear. He hated flying. He hated airplanes. As the stewardess reiterated the "preparation for landing" instructions, King heard the snap of laptops closing, the shuffling of papers being re-assembled and the click of briefcases being opened and closed. He both envied and loathed these people who could work completely relaxed on an airplane. How could anyone concentrate on a budget report or a spreadsheet at 35,000 feet, what with rises and plunges that would have frightened a roller-coaster engineer? The woman in seat

15A, with whom he had briefly shared comments about who got what space in the empty seat between them, had spent the entire flight absorbed in a novel about wolves devastating a small Russian village during a particularly hard winter in the early 20th century. She kept reading excerpts to him in flight. King clutched his airsickness bag the entire time, wishing he had a novel to distract him, but he couldn't read in motion, it just made him sicker. The plane bounced twice on runway 4 before the rear thrust from the wing baffles kicked in and King began to relax; a little. From the ramp, he raced to the men's room bumping into walls and other people with his bulky hand luggage. He never checked luggage, preferring to have everything he needed with him at all times, and he never, never, used the lavatory on an airplane. They were soo claustrophobic and he didn't like walking around on a floor that tilted and yawed at will. He washed his hands, splashed water on his face and checked his appearance in the mirror. He still looked pale and was trembling slightly. Maybe a sticky bun and a cup of coffee would get him back to the appearance of an FBI agent who had faced demons in the past. He was in Lucas's office by 11 am. If he hadn't shown his card, Lucas would have typed him as another shrink.

"Our lab agrees," he said. "Your female is either perfect, or from elsewhere, or it's one hell of a prank."

"Why did they pick you for this?"

King laid out his background. Law degree from Georgetown, Air Force staff with the Bureau of Unidentified Flying Objects ("A waste of time," he said), extensive work with the paranormal group at Duke (before it folded), assigned to follow the USSR research in telekinesis, back to headquarters when the Soviet bloc folded.

"So you believe this shit?"

"No, except for one time. Remember the exorcist priest who died in D.C. a decade ago? I was there for that. I couldn't find a rational reason for anything that happened then, so I believed him."

"So you limit yourself to Catholic demons?"

"Something happened there, and until someone shows me otherwise, I believe we were dealing with beings beyond our ken."

King paused, then said, "Sergeant, I don't get many cases, I'm not likely to be promoted, and I don't sleep well. I'm up here to put the kibosh on this thing and go home. I'm of a mind someone faked those chromosome prints."

"Impossible," said Devon. "I was there when they took the sample."

"Yeah, well, stranger things have happened."

"Not in Pittsburgh," said Lucas.

"Can you fill me in?" said King.

Lucas and Devon laid it out. Two things were sure: three chips were gone and there was the odd chromosome pattern. Suspects were few. Larry was the prime one and he might lead them to others; they had the list of hackers they were running down. Then things got murky: Miranda - if she existed; the angel Larry called Michael; who did Larry really have sex with; where the Excaliburs were; who wanted them and for what?

"Take Larry out of the equation and you have nothing," said King.

"You can try to break his story," said Lucas.

The officer opened the door to Larry's apartment. Lucas, King, and Devon walked in.

Larry was overwrought and kept murmuring, "It's my fault..."

Both Devon and Lucas were impressed with King's interrogation. He managed to calm Larry down, extract everything in a rational order, and get Larry's admiration and support.

"I want to help," said Larry.

"How can you help us?" asked King.

"I know the Excalibur. You get me near one and I can deactivate it."

"With what?"

"I have some bucky-tubes we're testing for their magnetic properties. The bar fits in the palm of my hand."

"How close would you have to get?"

"Within two feet."

"And what happens?"

"Lots of things, but basically the carbon atoms form a super-conductor that has a field strength of 80 gauss. That will alter the magnetic domains in the silicon and destroy the function of the chip."

"Aren't the chips worth millions? Would MicroFrame want that loss?"

"The chips can be replaced at modest cost. It's the architecture that's worth the money, and without a working chip they could never scope it out."

King humored him. "That's great, Larry. You stay here and we'll call on you when we locate the thieves."

"I told you he believes it," said Devon.

"Yeah, he's a dead end for now, but let's keep him handy. He's the only link we have," said King.

"I'm out of here," said Lucas. "I suggest we all get a good night's sleep so we're ready when the next angel feather falls."

Maria turned onto Forbes Avenue, looked into the rearview mirror, and said to the figure in the back, "You don't scare me anymore, not your threats nor your nightmares."

"I never tried to scare you, Maria. I wanted you to see the consequences of what you're doing. I have to convince you to stop."

"Why don't you just stop me yourself?"

"I have not been given that power."

"Even I could stop somebody if I tried."

"Humans were given free will, a blessing and a curse. You are allowed action in this realm. Angels are God's messengers; we can only act when He wills it."

"Heavenly eunuchs?"

"You cannot insult me. I have seen God."

"Ariel showed me Heaven and Hell."

"He showed you what you thought was so. He cannot attend Heaven. No fallen angel is allowed back."

"You're not even close to convincing."

"Move the car to safety and I will show you the possible."

Maria worried about doing anything this one said, but she found herself pulling over anyway. When they were parked it began.

It was not like the trip with Ariel. There was no sense of motion, only a sureness of being elsewhere. Michael and Maria stood on a hill, windswept, barren, like an eroded wasteland. In the valley below was a magnificent garden, lush, bountiful, every beast, bird, and insect roamed free. There were no humans.

Michael pointed to the single gate that led into the garden. This was guarded by a host of cherubim, each a vibrant blue, and each wielding a flaming sword.

"Man cannot return to the Garden until the day he completely defeats the Host of Evil," said Michael. "Then God will let His people in and they will dwell there for 1,000 years, knowing neither death nor hunger nor fear of any animal. When mankind has finished this sojourn he will be raised, triumphant, into heaven, where he will dwell closest to The Beatific Vision."

"Closer than the angels?"

"Yes, Maria. God loves man more than any of His other creatures. That made Satan envious and thus began his downfall."

"It doesn't bother you?"

"We have no earthly emotions. We neither laugh nor cry, nor have carnal desire."

"Don't you miss it?"

"We have bliss."

The scene before them disappeared, but Michael was not finished with their journey.

Now they were in a realm of light, soft, twilight blue; the air smelled of flowers.

"Watch now," said Michael. "The Apocalypse has been foretold."

An angel appeared before them and said, "Fear not. The time is at hand."

Trumpets sounded, seven golden candlesticks came into view, in the midst of which stood the Son of Man, He who was sent to redeem, the Godhead. He was clothed in a long white gown, cinched with a golden girdle; His hair and beard white, His eyes of flame. His feet were of burned brass, as if they were purified by fire, and He shone like the sun. In His right hand He held seven stars, which signified the seven religions of man. A two-edged sword came out of his mouth, to speak the truth in all directions.

When He spoke, it was as if the waters of the earth gave voice.

"I am the Alpha and the Omega," He said. "I am He that liveth, died, and lives evermore. Repent and you will eat of the Tree of Life in the midst of Paradise."

"I will forgive your sins, even those which mock Me, if only you but prostrate your soul. Fight the hour of temptation and I will make you a pillar in the temple of God."

Maria started to prostrate herself.

"Not now," said Michael. "This is a foretelling."

The figure spoke again. "Be not lukewarm, neither hot nor cold, or I will spit you out. But choose virtue and you will dwell in the New Jerusalem."

The sky opened around them and they were in a gilded hall. In the middle was a throne, a rainbow surrounding it, an emerald glow behind. Twenty-four seats, each with an Elder crowned with gold, flanked the throne. Seven lamps of the Spirit of God were set among them, and four beasts with many eyes and wings full of eyes, sat about the throne, singing a never-ending hymn of praise, "Holy, Holy, Holy, Lord God of Hosts, Heaven and Earth are full of Your Glory, Hosanna in the highest."

Michael and Maria stood on the crystal floor, while the Figure on the throne held out a book fastened by seven seals.

"Who can open the book?" He said.

No one came forward.

"This is the book of wisdom and justice. It must be opened to part the wicked from the good," the Figure said.

Then a lamb appeared, bleeding from wounds in its side. Harps played as the animal approached the book. The lamb knelt down, a cross cradled in one leg, and spoke.

"I have fulfilled the prophecies, Father. The world is ready."

The lamb broke the first seal and a white horse came forth with a conquering rider, to slay the unfaithful; the second seal evoked the red rider, who looked at Maria; the third rider, on a black horse, held balances on high and shouted, "Who will be measured?"

When the fourth seal was broken, Death entered and smiled at Maria. "You will know me," he said. The fifth seal revealed the souls who had died for Christ, all in white robes. The next seal unleashed a great earthquake and the sun turned black, the moon blood red. Four angels appeared, at the four corners of the earth, and held the winds, while another angel marked the heads of the faithful.

"They shall hunger and thirst no more, and God shall swallow up their tears," said a voice.

When the final seal, the seventh seal, was broken, a silence descended over heaven for 30 minutes. It was ended by the blare of seven trumpets played by seven angels, and when they blew, the earth was destroyed.

Just when Maria thought she could watch no more, a pregnant woman, clothed in the sun and standing on the moon, floated above the throne. At her feet was a crown of 12 stars, and as she stood she birthed the God Child.

Then Michael left Maria and led his angels in a battle with the dragon and his demons. The War of the Angels filled heaven with scenes of battle. Carnage was everywhere, but Maria knew that the central battle between Satan and Michael would decide the world's fate. The two magnificent foes appeared and filled the sky with their glory, the other angels watched. No image could equal what Maria saw before her; no words could describe its splendor. But it was the fight that surpassed all. It was as if the whole universe and all its energy were concentrated in this one battle. This clash lasted 20 minutes, each angel gaining advantage for a time. Then, with a great slash of his sword,

Michael smote his foe and stood astride the fallen Satan, his lance through the monster's chest.

"Cast him out, into the darkness," said the Lord.

And Satan was cast out, and with him the blasphemers who worshipped him.

Then a voice from the clouds said, "Fear God, and give glory to Him, for the hour of His judgment is come, and Babylon has fallen."

The wicked were gathered in a place called Armageddon, attended by angels who kept them imprisoned.

Then a white horse, mounted by a great Figure with many crowns on His head, pranced in front of the throne. On His thigh was written His name, "King of Kings and Lord of Lords." He sealed the Devil and his cohorts in Hell and welcomed the believers to His kingdom.

Then a new Heaven and Earth appeared, and a New Jerusalem came. The city had 12 gates through which the faithful entered. There was no need of sun or moon in this place because the Glory of God filled it with everlasting light and man would have night no more. And an endless chain of people, all robed in white, as far as Maria could see, chanted, "Glory to God in the Highest."

Maria and Michael were back in the car. Her head ached from the vision.

"That raised more questions than it gave answers," she said.

"You have seen enough. Be happy in your ignorance," he said, and then he was gone.

Maria was stretched to her limit and would ask no more today from either angel. She needed time to sort this out. Which angel was with God? Which was evil?

And where, where, where was Ariel?

17

Wednesday, December 19th

"How can I be sure who you are?" said Maria.

"I am a Seraph," Ariel responded.

"So? He says he's an Archangel."

"Look at the bruises on your cheek from the nightmare. Only a demon can do that."

"I need more. Let me see you as you truly are."

A smile crossed Ariel's face, her look more of bemusement than of aggravation.

"Maria, you are like Thomas, a doubter. If proof were given, what merit would there be in belief?"

"You know I'm being challenged by another," said Maria. "I want to follow you, but this is so important it confuses me."

"You will make the right choice. The evil he brings will not sway you, for you will know the truth."

Then Ariel lifted a few feet above the floor, standing on two winged wheels, each surrounding a small flame. Her countenance changed, an aura appeared about her face, the features like those of Matthew. The three other evangelists completed the ring about her head: Mark, to her right, his sign that of a Lion; to the left, Luke, the Ox; above, John, represented as an Eagle. A jade glow permeated the spaces between.

Two wings appeared above her head, cradling her face, which shone with a purple light. Her eyes were fixed beyond Maria, beyond this earth. Two other wings came out and folded around her legs. Then two wings from her side spread out and formed a covering for the light that emanated around her form. A gossamer web framed her from behind, setting her off from the room. Her space seemed different than the air in which Maria stood.

"The six-winged ones," muttered Maria, remembering her Bible stories.

The room was bathed in red, pink near the form of Ariel, and maroon at the edges. A hollow sound echoed off the walls, reminding Maria of a log drum she had heard played in Chichitenango. But it was the feeling of peace that emanated from the angel that soothed Maria the most. She started to speak, but instead fell into a swoon.

King sat in the chair near the window, staring out at the Point, where the Allegheny and the Monongahela met to form the Ohio River. He looked like a patient waiting for the receptionist to tell him the doctor was ready to see him. Lucas entered through the door that connected his office to the hall.

"We have a lead on the chip thief," he said.

Lucas ran his finger down the page of suspects and stopped at Karl Logsdon.

"This guy tells us that one of his e-mail buddies has entered a five-day hold on her mail. Her handle is 'Wirehead'. He says she's a wiz at complex circuits. We have to trace her entry point first. Apparently she's a recluse and has her mailbox run through a maze of aliases so no one can find her real address."

"Surely we can crack that."

"She's good, but we have our man working on it; says he'll have it in 24 hours."

"What about 'the speed of light' and all that stuff the ads for electronic mail tell us?"

"We're talking about a first-rate hacker. She's trying to conceal herself from other hackers. She knows how to hide."

But Lucas assured him that it was only a matter of a day and she'd be tracked down.

"What if she's not the one?" asked King.

"We haven't stopped the rest of our investigation, and we won't 'til we nail down the perpetrator."

"Can Larry help?"

"Maybe, if his bag is this Sherlock Holmes stuff," said Lucas.

"At the moment, we're as close to fingering the real thief as I am doing this." King pointed his finger at a random walker out near the Point. "What I want to know is how a computer jock got the skills of a cat burglar. We still haven't figured out how the chips got through security."

"Maybe they're still in the plant?" said Lucas.

"We're working on that, too. Everything's a possibility until a lead develops."

King pulled his chair up to Lucas's desk and started tossing theories out. Humble behavior for a Bureau man.

Maria stared at the algorithm for the connection sequence. If that failed, no chip, no matter how powerful, could access the power net. She worried about the residual problems of faulty circuits or overloaded lines at the terminal points. Routing tables and digital switching could also be insurmountable. But Ariel had assured her that accessing most of the video terminals was as good as getting all the terminals. Maria thought she'd get over 90%.

At Caltech, Maria had done a limited demonstration of the possibility of her system for her advisory panel by turning on eight terminals on the same circuit. By then TV sets no longer had the old mechanical turret tuners. Now, each set was never really "off" but kept in a low wattage state, the picture tube still charged. That was why long "warm-ups" were a thing of the past and why they could be accessed by the direct electrical signal Maria would send to them. But as difficult as her demonstration had been at Caltech, it looked woefully inadequate now. Tonight's test would try to access almost a million terminals in a 30-mile area. Quite a ramp-up by any standard. Friday night would mean at least three and a half billion sets worldwide. Numbers on a computer screen were one thing, but physical access to all those units was another. But the communications industry had helped. Over 120 million homes in the U.S. had cable modems; all those in Singapore did. They could handle 600 million bits per second, downloading a one-gigabyte file in a tenth of a second, assuring a brilliant image. On other sets it would be slower and not as clear, but still within acceptable limits. Bandwidths had increased 64-fold worldwide in the last two years. Channel switches were uniform, and auxiliary processors, like the V-chip, kept to established standards. Everything was in place. Once Ariel gave Maria the access codes, the transmission would be assured.

Maria flipped her Precision-Dot carbon-lead pencil back on the table, pushed her chair back, and wondered. A line from Shakespeare ran through her head: "Between the thought and the deed."

Bishop Cahill ignored the bells ringing noon, and listened carefully to what Father Malik was saying. He knew Malik was an expert on demons, and wished to reassure himself that the scholar before him hadn't lost a bean tramping about the woods near Uniontown. But Malik was sincere, fluent, learned, and compelling. Cahill wasn't convinced, but he saw no downside to letting the priest follow this lead. After all, it was only a few days.

"How can I be of help?" he said.

"Demons hate dealing with more than one person, Your Eminence. I need to keep you informed of my work so they know I am not alone."

Cahill assured him he would be there at any time.

"These cellular phones and such, though intrusive, can be useful at times. I'll even bring mine into church the next few days and put it on vibrate. Call if you need me."

Malik left the Bishop and went into the church. He genuflected in the middle aisle and knelt at the altar rail.

"God, if these things be true, help me to help this woman," he prayed. "And, I pray, keep her from harm."

Then he left for his rooms.

"Father," hissed the voice, making the word sound evil.

Malik started to leave the room, but heard the dead-bolt on the door slam shut. He saw the crucifix on the mantle and walked toward it. The voice laughed. Not a mirthful laugh, but one full of ominous foreboding. Malik wasn't getting closer to the mantle. It seemed to recede as he approached.

"Father," the voice hissed again, "you can't fight me."

Malik turned and saw the beast perched atop the chair, its body writhing as it talked.

"Angelus Satanae, ut me colaphizet," said Malik. [Messenger of Satan, sent to torment me.]

The beast laughed again, "Pope talk."

Malik remembered the cross around his neck and started to bring his right hand up to it. The hand moved slowly, as if it were in molasses.

"Destroyer," said the voice.

Malik's hand made it to the level of his chest. He tried to move it to the cross, but it kept going up. When it reached his face, the fingers splayed open, curling with their nails pointed outward. The nails sprouted, like a cat's, lengthening into curved scythes. Malik tried to pull the hand back down. It came closer.

"Dear God," said Malik. "Help me."

"Help you? Save you? Your arrogance is vapid. Who you call God deserts His people. He won't come to your call."

Malik brought his left hand up and grabbed his right wrist. The nails curled down and tore the skin above the knuckles. Blood poured out and down Malik's arm.

Then the right hand sprung open again, hurling the left hand away. Malik screamed. The nails on the thumb and pinky closed onto Malik's cheekbones, pinching his face forward. Then the three other fingers set themselves in his skin above the eyebrows and started pulling down. They sliced into his brows and anchored themselves in the tops of the eye sockets. Malik tried to scream again, but only a low gurgle passed his twisted lips.

All five fingers moved into a tight circle, cradling Malik's eyeballs. They pulled outward, dislodging the eyes into the hand without severing the optic nerves. Malik could see the skin below his cheekbones and the palm of the hand. His breathing was painful.

Now his left hand came up and pulled at the left eye. The right hand twisted the other eye so Malik could watch.

The beast laughed, "See how it's done."

The left eye reached the end of its tether. The hand pulled harder and the eye broke off, the nerve cord flopped onto Malik's cheek. The other hand let go.

Malik could see only the floor. The pain in his face was unbearable, but the beast kept him alert.

The phone rang five times; then the answering machine kicked in.

"This is Father Malik. I am not able to come to the phone at this time, please leave your message after the beep. God be with you."

The demon laughed again.

"Father, this is Maria Montez. I can't make it this afternoon. Are you free tomorrow before noon? You have my number, please confirm."

"Tomorrow?" said the fiend. "Would you like to live until tomorrow? I can arrange that."

Malik fell, his face slid along the floor, the eye draged alongside.

"You tortured us with your prayers and cantations," the voice said. "You will die slowly. Let me hear you pray the dark prayer."

"Never."

"Then you won't miss this."

Malik's hand jerked up and rammed into his mouth. The nails clasped onto the back of his tongue and dug into the tissue. Malik's cheeks fluttered as he tried to scream. The nails ripped at the flesh, twisting and pulling at the root of his tongue. He fell back against the wall.

"Pull!" shouted the beast.

Malik's hand yanked the tongue forward and severed it from his mouth. Blood poured down his throat. His hand held the tongue in front of his hanging eye, then threw it aside.

Malik lay panting, his eye rotated so he could see the mantle. The crucifix was gone. In its place was a large black cross and words on the mirror that read, "Worship Me, Priest."

"No!" thought Malik. "I will never worship you."

"Then, let's play, priest."

The fiend ran a nail down the priest's chest. "Now, now, which rib was it that He fashioned Eve from?"

He cut into the man's belly and tore out a rib. Malik was beyond pain, in a death-trance.

Then the demon turned the rib into the image of a Nun, demure, smiling. She glided to the stricken priest and took his mangled hand. She led him to an altar that appeared near the window.

"Lie with me, Father. Show your faithful how we fuck."

Malik was helpless; the Nun straddled him on the altar and pumped up and down on his engorged penis. Parishioners walked by the open window, scandalized at what they saw. Then the Nun shouted, "Deeper, deeper, Father, make me scream."

And scream she did when Malik exploded inside her. But she kept pounding until the priest was drained. Then she sat on his face and said, "Lick."

And the Nun was gone.

Then images of young men appeared and Malik began to stroke for them. He begged to stop but the Fiend just smiled.

"My, my, pity you hadn't done this before, deviant, " it hissed.

"Now will you worship me?"

"Never," croaked the Priest.

"Never? Not even in eternity? Ha!"

Malik tried to concentrate; to think of a way out.

The beast drove his nail into Malik's ribcage again and yanked out another rib. "How many of these do you have, Padre?"

"I will always curse you," said Malik.

"I have time to change your mind," said the beast. "Before the cock crows you will bend your knee to me."

18

Wednesday Afternoon

"I think we should tell her," said Rosa.

"We been through this," said Sal, "it's not worth the pain."

"But you see all those adopted kids looking for their parents. Why should Maria be kept in the dark?"

"This is different. The doctors at Pitt would have never worked with us if they thought we'd go public."

"Not public, just Maria. She can decide to go public herself."

"We can talk about it after our New York trip. I don' want to spoil that."

In 1966, Rosa and Sal were told they could never have children. Sal's sperm lacked the enzyme that dissolved the protective coating around the egg and allowed for penetration. Thirty-seven already, they faced a childless future.

Scientists at The University of Pittsburgh Medical School took them on as potential donors for their new test tube baby project. At a cost of $5,000 a pop, the Montezes tried six times to fertilize and successfully implant one of Rosa's eggs. They had no money to try again.

Doctor Moore took pity on the couple and convinced her colleagues to let them have a few more tries free of charge, partly because they were the only donors with this particular problem. On April 20, 1967, in her small laboratory in Scaife Hall, she manipulated one of Rosa's eggs under a microscope, gently scrapped away the outer layer with a micro-scalpel, and exposed it to a bath of Sal's sperm. The egg fertilized. She replaced the clear buffered solution with embryonic media from homogenized fetal tissue and serum from a fertile woman, antigen-screened to Rosa. Low levels of antibacterial and antifungal agents kept the media sterile. She placed the petri dish containing the egg into a chamber with sterile air and 5% carbon dioxide at human body temperature. The lights were turned off to give the room the darkness of a womb and to prevent any damaging photoproducts from forming.

That was the easy part. Eighteen days later, after watching the ball of cells in the dish divide through the blastula and gastrula stages of development, she inserted it into Rosa's uterus and waited. Unlike the other attempts, this egg anchored itself into the uterine wall. Once firmly attached, the cells sent appendages deep into the mother's tissue and began to siphon her life-giving blood. It grew.

After 30 days, no spontaneous abortion had occurred and hopes ran high. After 90 days, the pregnancy seemed successful. At term, the delivery room was full of expectant scientists and Sal. Maria was born at 4:06 PM on January 13, 1968.

"A miracle," said Rosa.

Because of possible public criticism, especially from the large Catholic population of Pittsburgh, and because the Montezes were Catholic themselves and wanted to avoid any discussion of their motives, everyone keep their silence. Moore referred to the child as Helen Lane, and a modest report was published in Reproductive Physiology, with special permission to allow aliases for the researchers. Later successes would receive full media attention.

Maria was accorded free medical care by the staff at the hospital under a private agreement with the Mellon Foundation that had funded the research. Her normal progress was well documented, and the results were sealed from access except to the Montezes and in case of medical emergency.

Rosa wanted to name the child Mercedes, "the gift", because she was so special. Sal wanted a simple name. They both agreed to invoke the Virgin of Guadalupe. So, Maria Mercedes Montez blossomed into adulthood.

"I just think it's only fair to her," said Rosa.

"I said later," Sal raised his voice. "We can discuss it then."

But others knew of the gift-child, followed her progress, kept her from harm.

Maria picked up the phone on the second ring.
"We need to talk before we go with your parents," said John. "How about lunch at Heinz Field?"
"The football stadium?"
"Yeah, the premium restaurant is great and the Steelers will be practicing."
God, ever the boy, she thought and smiled.

Handling John might prove difficult. Maria made it through college determined not to "find a husband," much to her mother's dismay. Graduate school changed that. She met John at a party, and was attracted by his laid-back attitude, charm, and humor, and he wasn't a tech-nerd. They were soon dating. Inertia led to marriage and, in the early days, love.

John finished a Masters of Fine Arts in painting, but needed time to develop his potential. None of the works from his thesis, "Christian Symbolism in Modern Art," sold. His graphic design business was mostly a day job. He wanted his paintings to support them. To Maria's surprise, he also wanted children.

"We have our careers to get started," said Maria.
"We could fit in children," said John.
"Later. I'm not throwing away all my training the first chance I get. Besides, we need my salary to get a good start."
Maybe Maria was right, a few years to get a leg-up and a family after that. But then they were 32 and Maria was

appointed lab director. She was pleased that people noted how remarkable that was for one so young. As their salary gap widened, so did the gulf between them.

"Things are going well," she said.

"For you, not me."

"Well, if you'd change a little, they might go well for you, too."

"Change? How?"

"Your paintings are too dark and depressing. They scare everybody," said Maria. "Who wants to be reminded of Judgment Day?"

"I'm surprised you even noticed."

"Well, it's obvious."

"So, you're an art critic, too?"

"I'm trying to help."

John brought up children again.

"Not now, maybe not ever," said Maria.

Things went downhill from there. Maria worked long hours, traveled constantly, was cranky when she was home. Mix that in with John's inherent calm and imperturbability, all of which she blamed on laziness, and the fact that her parents seemed to like him better than her, and the issue came to a head.

Maria walked into John's studio, planted her feet, dropped her hands to her waist, and said, "If you must paint, why not paint what people will buy?"

"I don't tell you what to do at work," he replied.

"Damn right you don't. My career is booming. You're going nowhere."

"Don't start. Advertising is my front. I put my creativity into my paintings. Besides, we have enough."

"Supplied by me. We both want that house in Fox Chapel and could afford it if you contributed more."

"What good's that big house? I don't hear the pitter-patter of little feet around here."

"We should be well off by now, in the market, with a nest egg."

"It's come to money?"

"No. I expect ambition, some spunk, drive."

"Shut up!"

Maria was out of the house and in the car before she knew it. She drove to the mall, walked a few laps, then went home.

"We have to talk," she said.

The end of the marriage.

They met in the lobby. Maria complimented John on how good he looked.

"My stuff is selling all of a sudden. Who knows how long it will last."

"I'm getting to believe you should just enjoy the moment. What is it the Marines say? 'Harpe Diem'?" she said.

"It's 'Carpe Diem'."

"Oh."

"Maria, how will we manage this weekend?"

"It sounds enjoyable. We used to like dinner and dancing."

"No, it's not that. I can handle us being with them when we ignore each other, but this cooperative mood of yours throws me."

"I can change."

"You never wanted to. Are things going well for you at work?"

"Actually, I'm into the most exciting work of my career."

"Don't tell me about it, I wouldn't understand."

"You will when it's over."

"Huh?"

"Nothing. Yes, you're right; we should set up some guidelines. I don't want to get Rosa started again about us, but I want them, especially Sal, to really enjoy themselves."

"Why don't we pretend we're dating, not reconciling?"

"That should work. Whatever you say."

"Whatever I say? Maria, are you all right?"

"Heavenly."

John ordered drinks. Then Maria asked how his work was going.

"Have you been to the Carnegie?"

"I never have time."

"Well, I have an exhibition there now. The turning of the 5th World is very good for my work."

"That's right. It would be. I saw a painting of yours at Saint Joseph's."

"You're going to church again?"

"No. I just had some business there."

John had one eye on Maria, the other on the quarterback who had just hit a receiver with a bullet pass. His lack of attention was a turn-on.

The waiter brought the lemon oil salads and they started eating. Over the lamb, Maria said, "You know, with a little help and some luck we could have made it."

"No, Maria, your work is your life. Just face it and you'll stay content."

"Maybe content isn't enough. I'm getting to feel I want more."

"Children?"

"I haven't pursued it that far, but it's possible. I just don't know yet, but I'm feeling like a new era is starting in my personal life."

"Don't rush it. There are no real goals in life, just destinations. And you don't have to reach those, just be pointed in the right direction."

"You always had a simple philosophy."

"It keeps me level. I don't go for the 'A man's reach should exceed his grasp' bullshit. That only leads to frustration."

"But are you happy, John?"

"Reasonably."

"Anyone else?"

"Some distractions, nothing serious."

"That's what I need. Distractions."

They finished and left, neither saying goodbye.

Maria wondered where her sense of calm was coming from. Here she was, on her way to Elaine's, chasing the wildest project anyone had ever had, and she was humming show tunes. It was time for the mood doctor, for sure, but not until Monday.

Elaine had cleaned up her apartment.

"I don't know what came over me," she said. "The work went so fast, I had some free time, and I felt like getting this place in shape. I think it was having that guy in here yesterday. He scared the shit out of me, but when he left I kept thinking I should red up the place in case he ever returned."

"I think he's seen worse."

"Don't you like it?"

"Yes, Elaine, it's great. You're getting cleaner, I'm driving around singing, leaving behind a mess at my place, my parents are happy with me, and I just had lunch with John. Carpe Diem."

"Don't go odd on me, Boss. This ship we're building needs an anchor."

"Yeah, I'll be the fuckin' anchor.... Oh, I'm sorry, Elaine, it just came out."

Elaine looked at Maria with a curious eye. This pillar of science was slouching into a lab freak.

And there on the newly scrubbed bench was The Savior. As messy as Elaine could be about personal things, she was meticulous in her work. The Savior gleamed. No loose ends, bent junctions, burrs to cut your hand. No, it was a thing of beauty, like a hand-cut jewel, a luster radiating from the reflected light. Maybe when they were done the Metropolitan would want it for an exhibit.

"Boss? Elaine to Maria?"

Maria snapped to. "Does it work?"

"Should, but how can we tell if we don't test it?"

Maria hefted The Savior in her hand. The motherboard weighed almost nothing; add to that the switching circuitry, the telemetry, the mechanical support, the program driver, and the whole thing was 4 ounces. Then there were the cable and the shielding, the packing material, and the safety overrides, and still it was no heavier than a camera.

"It'll work on any outlet?" asked Maria.

"Yep. Fifty to 250 cycles; 20-500 volts You could use it abroad."

"How did you clean the stage?"

"Lemon juice. Works as well as the old CFCs."

"Suppose there's a power surge or an open circuit when we plug it in?"

Elaine pointed to the strip connector. "Allowed for," she said.

"We have to be sure."

"That's what the test is for."

"Will we have time to redesign it if it doesn't work?"

"You won't have to; it will work," said Elaine. "If it doesn't, you don't have to pay me."

"It's not the money, Elaine. I just have to be sure. I'll run a few more checks now and then we'll be ready. Ariel will be over about 10."

"Does she just fly over?"

"I assume. Why don't you ask her?"

"Like she'd tell me, eh?"

"Who knows what she'd do? We're the tools, she's the maker. She tells us what she wants when she wants."

Maria picked The Savior up again. "Why toggle switches?"

"When you want to be sure one time, you use the old mechanical stuff."

"The output cable looks like it could be dropped from an airplane and still connect."

"Taking no chances."

"Three pilot lights?"

"If all three don't light, we have a problem. I know there's no redundancy in the chip, but the simple things need it."

"It's built like a weightless tank."

"I'll be carrying it in my pouch, and I don't want any screw-up from my end."

"Your end's *the* end," said Maria.

"Oh, no. You're the leader, Elaine follows. I don't want the responsibility."

"You don't know how wise you are."

"Who we got tracing Wirehead?" asked Lucas.

"Snoopy," said Traynor. "He's the best we know. He already knows she uses a screen in Chicago. Want to meet him?"

Snoopy was Shinto Ito, physicist by training, computer security cop by trade. "When they shut down Oak Ridge, I looked elsewhere. I didn't even know I had this gift until I got burned by a hacker myself."

"How much longer 'til we find her?"

"A day, two at most. It depends on what type of firewall she's built to protect against intruders. I'll try to outflank her to get an outbound destination port. If she's here it will make it easier, but my stuff is portable, it can go anywhere."

"You using the Service?" asked King.

"Don't need it. No insult intended, but I don't need a bureaucracy weighing me down."

"No insult taken, but if you ever want to get inside..."

Ito held up his hand. "Never happen. If I can't do this, I'll just retire or run my own consulting company."

Ito called up a map of the U.S. and Canada on his screen. He showed the two men the path he had traced so far. Toronto - Edmonton ("she uses four different routers there") - Seattle - White Sands ("She set a trap there.") - San Diego - Austin ("The IP link dropped.") - Chicago.

"None of this is a problem for her with satellites, but she's super careful."

"Could she be foreign?"

"She could be Venus rising from a clamshell, but why guess? We'll know soon."

Back in Lucas's car, they talked of waiting.

"It drains the adrenaline more than the chase."

"It *is* the chase, when you think of it," said King. "You focus on something for days and all of a sudden the solution pops into your head. I've had it happen when I was sleeping."

"Intuition?"

"No, I think the brain just unravels the jumble of bits of information that are coming in and sees the pattern. It almost never fails."

"I know," said Lucas. "I often don't tell anyone how I figure things out. I'm afraid they'd think I'm crazy."

"Well, we'll have to be loony to scope this one down to size."

Lucas went back to the station and checked on the men working the list; King returned to his hotel for a nap.

Lucas and Devon, with Larry in tow, came to King's room.

"I think I know what they want to use the Excaliburs for," said Larry.

"Who?" asked King.

"I don't know who, just what."

"Go ahead."

"The game is about power. How many people can you control? We don't need standing armies if we can access people in their homes, at work, in their cars, wherever. Marx and Engels knew that and it was Lenin who said that thing about controlling the means of communication."

Larry went on to tell them how he could packet-sniff anyone's e-mail, listen in on their communications, determine to whom they talked, and, in a few days, give them a complete profile of the individual, from the checks he wrote, the medicines he ordered, and the appointments he made, to what socks he wore, where he wore them, and what he viewed on the Internet. He could use simple power lines, TV cables, phone lines; pick transmissions out of the air.

"How much of this is legal?" asked King.

"You don't know? The Feds have the Clipper Chip which gives you the 'keys' to decode conversations. And you guys are in court trying to stop the PGP antidote."

Larry then told of industry's push to get to the information junction first so they could talk to billions of people at once.

"Think of your video screen as a window," he said. "Every time you look out, you give them an opportunity to look in."

In answer to their questions, Larry said, "To sell things, to catch criminals, to influence voters, to lead the flock. Privacy is gone."

He described the German InfoBahn, a wireless network designed to log onto all of Europe. "If that works, who's to stop them in the future from accessing the world? No one would be off-line except in places like North Korea, where there are no satellite links, fax machines are illegal, and all information comes from one source. That's negative control."

Then he explained that receiving information, though powerful, was peanuts compared to transmitting it. As people became more and more dependent on video input, they became more susceptible to control from outside.

"Now the remote terminals you access can be simple. Even an ancient P3 would work for detailed messages, and a simple TV for video signal. It's at the transmitting end that you need something huge, and that could be the Excalibur."

The three men looked stunned. "When could this start?" asked Lucas.

"Come on! Are you really that out of touch? Have you wasted all your effort trying to stop cyberporn? You've never been part of a video conference on the Internet? Don't you know that some of us send information to our homes to regulate energy use, start the oven, and respond to environmental changes like heat or pollution? My crummy apartment is sensing the air quality right now and determining whether to pulse the exhaust fan."

Then Larry ticked off all the subtle but concrete ways that signals were already controlling lives. He told of genetic algorithms that allowed computer codes to change their own form and evolve in response to feedback from electro-sensors which counted the input from side branches, and how every item people bought had an imbedded sensor that could be traced at any time.

"You know, people think guys like me are out of touch, lost in our own little world. Well, our world *is* the world. We're not the ones wearing blinders. Some day you'll wake up and find yourself lost in details you didn't even know existed."

"What would 'they' want to transmit?" asked Devon.

"I don't know, but I bet it's big."

"Can you find her, Larry?" asked King.

"I haven't been trying, but, yes, I can do it."

They told him about Snoopy.

"I know the guy. Not bad, but I can do better. I just usually have more important things to do."

"Then stay with us. We'll get Ito over to show you how far he's gotten and you can take it from there."

"My pleasure," said Larry, who began to smile. "Snoopy meets Peanuts."

"Peanuts?"

"My first handle. When I was eleven."

19

Wednesday Night

The storm approached Pittsburgh from the west, coming up over the airport, passing PNC Park and Heinz Stadium, and spreading across the Point. The air crackled from the pent up charge massed in the thunderheads. The first bolt of lightning hit the US Steel Building, raced down its outer core of oxidized metal and spread into the ground. Once the ion channels were established, huge ground strokes shot up, their flash patterns giving the appearance of coming down from the clouds. The little downtown church nestled among the skyscrapers appeared black against the pulsing silver sky. Every transmission tower in a 15 mile area was hit by at least one stroke, some exploding the fuse boxes, others jumping the fuse and burning holes in the earth.

Tall trees were special targets, escaping permanent damage if the current ran along the outside bark, or exploding inside and burning even before the bark melted. In some places there were 30 strokes every few minutes. Over Fox Chapel, lightning leapt from cloud to cloud, never touching the ground. The charged air was extended and bolts appeared in places where the storm hadn't reached. The thunder pattern was so intense that people couldn't determine which clap went with what stroke.

The Pittsburgh Plate Glass complex of green mirrored buildings, which earlier had twinkled like Oz, now looked like a gigantic haunted house, white and silver bolts attracted to its high towers. Glass held rigidly in frames broke under the changes in pressure, raining pieces of pane as large as posters on the streets below. Within minutes the central plaza was covered with tons of shattered windows, as if a bomb had gone off. So much lightning hit the Point bridges that they looked like cages from Frankenstein's lab.

Elsewhere, people cowered inside their homes, hoping the storm would pass. Airplanes swerved to avoid the storm. One about to land reported the appearance of ball lightning inside the cabin. The blue green ethereal blob hovered in the air and wobbled back and forth above the heads of the frightened passengers.

When the rain clouds hit they dropped water in sheets. Sewers, unable to handle the surge, backed up and flooded the streets. Shadyside was under water, Lawrenceville streets awash. Cars parked in low areas were submerged; downed power lines arced out, shutting off electricity to many homes. Wind blew the rain horizontal, lashing at windows and leaking around doors. Even the lights at Elaine's flickered.

"We don't need this," said Maria.

"It will not harm us," said Ariel. "It has been sent."

"Well, then, can you call it off?" asked Elaine.

"It provides a diversion for your test."

Maria caught Elaine's eye. No more questions of Ariel.

Elaine's place had four distinct power circuits. Plugged into one was an old TV, showing Channel 5; another had Elaine's TV in the off position; the third was an old Pentium machine, running a Windows' program; the last had two monitors running off one sub-station, also turned off. Two portables, one on, one off, sat on the side bench.

Elaine looked at Maria. "Ready when you are."

Ariel returned Maria's glance with a nod. Maria closed her eyes and threw the toggle switch. The three red lights blinked on.

The three sets that were already on responded first, showing the display Elaine was filming with her video cam. In seconds the other sets warmed up and broadcast the same signal.

"Whoopie!" said Elaine.

"Thank God," said Maria. "Thank God."

"Someday you will receive your thanks directly from Him," said Ariel. "Now know that you are doing the Lord's work."

They let the signal run for 20 seconds then shut Savior down. The sets either shut off or returned to their previous screens. Maria sighed; Elaine walked about punching things.

They both turned to see if Ariel was pleased, but she had gone.

"Here display, gone tomorrow," said Elaine.

"We have our orders for tomorrow," said Maria. "I guess that's enough for her."

"Next time can we get a more chummy leader?"

"I can't believe it really worked. I always thought it was a long shot, and that I was awarded my Ph.D. because they couldn't properly test my theory. Now, to see it in action, what a rush!"

"You're assuming the rest of the town received this?"

"Oh, yeah. I forgot. But Ariel would have stayed if there were a problem."

"I have a way to test."

Elaine dialed a number. "Me... Elaine. Sorry to bother you, but I just had a weird signal on my screen... Yeah, like that... You too?... Know what it was?... If you find out, let me in on it... Thanks."

"It made it to Aliquippa," said Elaine.

"We're on!"

20

Thursday, December 30th

The front page of the morning Pittsburgh Post Gazette was full of descriptions of the storm and its damage. Buried on page 14 was an item that read:

Curious Interruption of TV Transmissions

In an odd aside to the storm damage, people all over the area reported interruptions in their TV programming. At about 10:47 P.M., TV sets turned on in many homes and, in addition to those already on, displayed a Test Pattern, much like those used when stations go off the air. People working late at their computer terminals reported the same phenomenon.

Ethan Hunter, professor of physics at Pitt, said,

"We know very little about lightning. It's possible the storm caused this." "Nonsense," said professor Aidan Owens of the Carnegie-Mellon computer science Lab. "This wasn't caused by any lightning." When asked what did cause the interruptions, he replied, "Some nitwit is tinkering with the communications system."

Although local police dismissed the incident, federal officials have asked anyone who was recording at the time to please send the tape to them for analysis. The address is:

FCC, 1020 Pennsylvania Avenue North West, Washington, D.C. 20006.

"I told you," said Larry. "That was a test."

"How long to track the source down?" asked Lucas.

"Maybe a week, but you don't have that long. You run a test like this right before you use it, to escape detection. I expect a real run soon."

"Does this mean our hacker is in Pittsburgh?"

"Looks like it," said Larry. "Why else run the test here?"

"So Pittsburgh is the target?" asked King.

"Why limit it to that? If they can do Pittsburgh, they can do far more," said Larry.

Devon spoke. "Larry, please think hard. Have you talked to anyone about the Excalibur?"

"No way. It's mine."

"I thought as much. And you're still sure no one could wire it in without the blueprints?"

"I didn't think so. But with this TV stuff all bets are off. The Excalibur was used last night."

"You're sure?"

"I've run a line assay on the Tivo in my TV; the signature is there."

Lucas's office door flew open. It was Ito.

"Our hacker is here, in Pittsburgh. She initiates at the SteelCity interface. We spoofed past her security locks and found her in the directory of a little used account. The account owner says he hasn't used it in weeks, but last night it transmitted over 200 terabytes."

"What's next?"

"I have a tech driving around hoping she activates her modem. He has a frequency detector linked to a laptop. When she logs on we have her."

Larry and Ito planned the next step. The phone rang.

"Sergeant Lucas," said the voice. "We're down to two names; one should be your suspect."

"How soon?"

"Half hour."

"Give me both of them now."

Elaine packed The Savior in a polystyrene container the size of a Kleenex box. She placed this in a black overnight bag, added 30 feet of 10 gauge shielded wire with a lightning proof plug at one end and a male connector at the other. The bag was surrounded on the inside by a metal Faraday cage to prevent disturbance by outside electric fields in transit.

What looked like a normal zipper was, in fact, a steel locking retainer that ran around the outside of the bag. The bag handles were reinforced with flexible steel loops and anchored into the fabric with wide platform catches. It looked much like a pilot's small carry-on case.

Elaine was not traveling with Maria. To avoid airport security, she drove the seven hours to Manhattan and checked into the Roger Smith Hotel on 49th and Lexington. The bellhop gave a little smirk when he lifted, over Elaine's objections, the small overnight bag and the almost weightless suitcase containing Elaine's clothes. She tipped him a dollar.

"Open up, Miss Masters!" shouted the officer, pounding the door. "This is the last time we ask before we force our way in."

No response. He signaled the pick-man who came forward and started on the lock. It opened in 20 seconds.

"Anyone home?" he called.

No reply. They scanned the studio, the work bench cluttered with parts. The piece of paper Maria had used to draw the system caught their notice. Two blocks on the flow diagram were labeled EX.

"Call it in," he said. "We have our thief."

"How long?" asked Lucas, looking about the small apartment.

"Hard to tell. No established pattern of meals, no phone records except the one call. Owner says he has no idea where she is, usually stays home. I'd say she left within eight hours, maybe less," said the officer.

"Stake it out. Call us if she comes back."

But Lucas didn't think she'd be back, at least not in time. He called in to headquarters and asked for a transit search. In two hours they had her toll booth receipts and times. She was in the New York area.

Maria was in Point Breeze, helping her parents get ready. That consisted mostly of removing things from Rosa's bags.

"You won't need four pairs of shoes," said Maria. "And you should stop wearing heels." She thought, "You only wobble in them anyway, at your weight."

"I need them, just in case," replied Rosa.

"She thinks of me as a burro," said Sal. "If she ever carried her own bags, she'd learn."

"Why not give her the chance?" said Maria.

Sal looked at his daughter with a confused glance. Where had he gone wrong?

"Never mind, Dad, let's just get this ready."

Sal coughed up some phlegm into his handkerchief, wiped his mouth, and wondered why Maria was staring at him so hard. She turned in disgust, walked into the kitchen and called Malik again. He didn't answer. *Huh, wasn't he the one who said they should work together?* And now she was off to New York and he was God knows where.

John came over at 12:30. He would leave his car in their drive and they would all go to the airport together.

"Why should we pay two parking fees?" asked Sal.

"Your father's a great guy," said John to Maria when they were alone. "Spends $6000 for dinner tickets and cheaps on the parking."

"It's his training."

"I meant it as a compliment."

"Will you drive? Sal's so hopped up he's primed for a cardiac."

"If he lets me. I'm still a teenager to him."

"I know, the son he never had."

It was 2:00 P.M. when they got to the priest's residence. King and Lucas knelt near the body. The torment on the dead face frightened them both. How a man could pull his own eyes and tongue out was beyond them. Did the priest masturbate before he killed himself? Why were his knees scraped and bloody, his testicles strewn over the floor?

"Who did this?" asked King?

"CSI say it was him, no other prints, no nothing. They're convinced he was alone. What kind of crappola is that?. How could anyone not pass out when mutilating himself like this?"

"CSI my ass," said King. "Unless it's some paranormal thing we don't know about, this was caused by others. Could it be connected to our chip thief?"

"Maybe. That's why I came over when I heard the rumors going through the precinct. I mean if we're dealing with the supernatural and this guy is an expert...," said Lucas.

"This means they've turned violent."

"Right. Unless they find traces of hard drugs in his sample, he must have been tortured by something else."

"Like what," asked King?

"Something more fiendish than anything I know about."

"Captain, I have his schedule," said the officer.

Lucas leafed back through the appointment book. Yesterday, only Bishop Cahill at noon, before the priest died; Tuesday only a Maria Montez; Monday, nothing. They went over to the answering machine and retrieved the Montez messages.

"Can you estimate when the woman's calls were?"

"Done that through the phone company. The first call was yesterday afternoon, the second one about 11 A.M. today."

"We'll check her out," said Lucas.

"It's that he was an expert in demonology that worries me," said King.

"Sure. Larry and his visitors, and now this priest. We'll check all his appointments for the week until we find one that clicks."

Bishop Cahill said a lot. Yes, Father Malik had felt he might be on the trail of a demon. No, he hadn't mentioned the woman's name. Yes, it was a rush job, Malik had even called Rome for permission. No, Malik was no fool.

The Maria Montez in the phone book wasn't answering. Her landlord connected them to Infinity. No, she wouldn't be in again for a week, but they had her parents' number on file as next of kin on her insurance policies.

The Montezes didn't answer either, but their neighbors, the Logans, knew they were off to New York, and even knew the name of the travel agent they used. They thought Maria was with them, but they weren't sure.

"Christ, a computer wiz. No record, not even a jaywalking ticket. Admired at work, the girl next door at home. Who the fuck is she?" asked Lucas.

"Here they are, four seats together," said the agent. "Flight left at 2:45 this afternoon, landed in La Guardia at 4:05."

"Hotel?"

"We didn't book it, but I know it's in Manhattan."

"Where do they usually stay in New York?"

"First trip I've ever booked for them there, and I've been their agent for twenty-six years."

Lucas and King went outside.

"Any sense our staying here?" said Lucas.

"Nope. The Masters woman is in the New York area; so is Montez. We need Larry, of course, and Devon in case Larry ping-pongs on us."

"Think this will hold over the weekend?" asked Lucas.

"You're not serious?"

They finished up their reports and booked the morning flight to Newark.

21

Thursday Evening

The Benjamin Hotel, 50th and Lexington, catty-corner to the Waldorf-Astoria, suite 2203. Sal Montez wanted the family to be together.

"Which is my room?" said Maria.

John answered first. "Why don't I take the living room? The couch looks fine and I can use the bathroom in the smaller bedroom."

Sal waited for Maria to offer. She didn't.

"And Maria can take the small room with the double bed," Rosa emphasized.

"First come see our room," said Sal, ushering them into a large room with a California King bed and a patio off the French doors. The view was to the south.

"I'll be cookin' one meal a day," said Rosa, marching around the small kitchen. "You're on your own for the rest."

It was awkward, everyone in one suite, but the Montezes preferred that to separate rooms, and they were paying.

When Maria was in her room, she called the Roger Smith. "Miss Hudson's room please?"

Elaine answered. "Went fine, no delays. I've checked The Savior out and it's perfect. I'll wait for your next call."

"I'll figure out an excuse for the morning. Be at your door by ten."

"Our marriage is dead," Maria said to her mother, who came in to ask her why she hadn't offered John her room. "Don't try to force us together again."

"We never forced you to do anythin'!" said Rosa. "That was our mistake."

Maria let it go. She had bigger things on her mind, and the cover her parents were providing was perfect.

"We have the place for three nights," said Sal. "And it's a short hop from here to the Rainbow Room tomorrow. We can even walk if there are no cabs."

"Not in heels," said Rosa.

They wanted a New York experience, so the concierge suggested a deli on 11th Street. After that it was a drink at the Top of the Sixes, where they could look down on the new high-tech message board that replaced the old "Zipper" as it rotated the news ticker around the Times Square Building. How many people had gotten their first notice of

VE Day, VJ Day, the death of Kennedy, from that sign? And how many would watch it tomorrow?

"What was the best message you ever seen?" Sal asked the waitress.

"I don't know," she replied. "Maybe the last one, 'I am going to the Museum of the City of New York. Visit me there on May 18. The Zipper.'"

Two drinks, then back to the Benjamin for the night.

22

Friday Morning
December 21, 2012

The Coming of the 5th World

Getting away from her folks was no easy task. She needed John.

"Please, I just need some excuses for today," she said.

"I don't want to lie to your parents."

"I'll make it up to you, I promise."

"You can't make it up to me."

"One damn day! Have I ever begged you for anything before?"

"No, so why the change? What the hell is going on with you?"

"I promise, give me some free time today and I'll never ask again."

"I don't like being around you anymore."

"Good, I'll be scarce if you just give me an out."

"The Circle Line? A bit cold for a boat ride, don' you think?" said Sal. "Maybe we'll join you."

Rosa pulled on his sleeve.

"You kids go ahead, we have stuff we wan' to do around the hotel," Sal said.

They parted, John off to the "War and Destruction" exhibit of Anselm Kiefer's paintings at MOMA. They would meet back in the lobby at one.

Maria went down the block to the Roger Smith. "Room 1411," said the clerk. She took the elevator up to Elaine's room.

They went over their plans one more time and then cabbed it to the Times Square Building on 42nd Street. The driver let them off across the street. As they started to cross, a pickup swerved toward them, missing them by a few feet.

"What the hell was that?" asked Elaine.

"He was trying to kill us. I saw his eyes; he was in some kind of trance."

"Well, thanks for saving my life," said Elaine.

"It wasn't me. I didn't do anything."

"Then who did?"

Ariel stepped forward. "Follow me."

They walked straight into the traffic, toward the entrance to One Times Square. Drivers slammed their brakes, cabs stopped, a bus waited. No horn blared. People stared at the event; a woman crossed herself and murmured, "Like the parting of the Red Sea."

Ariel left and traffic resumed as if nothing had happened.

Elaine went to the small kiosk near the building's entrance and bought a copy of Computer World, unfolded six crumpled dollar bills she pulled from her jeans, and placed them flat on the counter.

The two women signed into the building as Hudson and Jenkins, flashing fake IDs at the bored guard. "Some people never take a day off," he said, pointing to the elevator. They went up to the offices of Evans and Sons, Tax Consultants, on the 22nd floor. They slid the key Ariel had given to them into the lock, but the door opened before they turned the knob.

"Who are you?" asked Maria.

"I am Miranda. I work with Ariel."

"Dressed like that?"

Miranda smiled. "This is an important day in your space. Everyone is ready to party, and I must look the part."

"I wouldn't let any of the men you meet get too close."

"I have control over myself and others."

"I'll bet," said Elaine.

"Why hasn't Ariel mentioned you?" asked Maria.

"Please, no questions," said Miranda, who got right down to business. First she warned them about Michael. "He's about, and he has his demons with him. They will do anything to stop us."

"He just tried to kill us downstairs."

"I know. He will try again up here. He wants to take control of the roof."

She showed them around the small suite, then took them up the two floors to the roof.

At the top of the stairs, Maria asked, "They leave this door open?"

"They ran a test of the World Ball this morning; another is planned for 6, and then they arrive at 11 for the celebration. The door is locked, but I can open or secure it at will. Lucifer will try to stop us, but you just be brave. We will prevail."

"What do we do with the people running the show at 11?"

"They are my consideration. Everything is planned. Elaine will be with me, and you will come with Ariel. Do not be afraid. We will take care of each detail."

Elaine checked the power plugs with her multimeter. Voltage 115, current 20 amperes. Just what she expected. They had a choice of four outlets. "Any preference, Boss?"

"No, just keep the videocam on a separate circuit from The Savior in case one fails. We can use that light grey wall for a backdrop, unless Ariel thinks otherwise." Then in a whisper to Elaine and with an eye on Miranda she said, "Don't trust this one."

Maria leaned over the edge and looked at the street. Broadway and Seventh Avenue met at 45th Street, then splayed out on either side. The effect was of an enormous bowtie. Maria wondered if New York had planned it that way.

It reminded her of the drawing from the book Father Malik had given her of the Valley of Armageddon. She quoted from the Apocalypse for Elaine, "For they are the spirits of devils, gathered to do battle on that great day of God Almighty, in a place called Armageddon."

"Just imagine all those people down there tonight. What a show we'll give them," Maria said.

"What's in the show?" asked Elaine.

"Ariel, and others whom I haven't met, are going to stop Satan from broadcasting his evil tirade tonight. The Savior will give us the access we need for worldwide reception. Then the good angels will broadcast their message. They'll show love and hope and virtue. The things that drive the Devil mad. It's how we will defeat him this time."

Elaine picked out a spot for filming and set up the tripod.

"You're not going to leave me with her?" she asked.

"For a while. Just don't tell her anything," said Maria.

"I suppose you're not cold," she said to the scantily clad Miranda.

Then they left the roof and went back downstairs.

Miranda handed Maria the access codes, arranged alphabetically by country. Maria went over to Savior and installed the backwards driver she and Elaine had programmed to decipher them. She typed her code from Infinity, activated the program, and saw her password appear on the screen. Good. Then she started keying in the country codes. When all 197 were entered, she turned to Elaine.

"Check for mistakes."

Elaine ran the check. "Looks good to me."

Maria sat down in front of the screen and Elaine read the codes to her as she scrolled them by.

"Good. I hope no major country makes changes tonight."

Elaine settled back on the couch. She planned a limited test of Savior on the video monitors in the office. "Just to be sure." She was to stay in the office until the run.

Maria was rolling her hands over each other, wishing it were midnight. Then she walked to the door.

"Won't they know Elaine hasn't left?" she asked.

Miranda transformed into Elaine. "Let's go," she said, in Elaine's voice.

Elaine started whistling and backed into the corner.

The woman and the angel signed out and left the building. Miranda took her leave and Maria took the Shuttle over to Grand Central, transferred to the Lexington Avenue line, and got off at 51st Street. She walked the half block to the Benjamin, and entered the hotel at 1:06. She waited in the coffee shop, picking a stool that gave her a view of the lobby. John was 20 minutes late.

They called up for Sal and Rosa, who came down for lunch.

"We could eat in the room," said Rosa.

"No," said John. "I know an Afghani restaurant near the 59th Street Bridge I'd like to take you to."

The cab ride took seven minutes and cost seven dollars. Maria knew the omen in that number.

Over Bethlehem, Pennsylvania, the Boeing 757 turned from NorthEast to due East; the four men pensive in their aisle 11 seats as they approached Newark. King tried to hide his airsickness. The stewardess came down the aisle, asking for Captain Lucas. He raised his hand.

She told him the cockpit had been contacted with a message for him. He had forgotten to turn his cell back on after take-off. She offered him the co-pilot's phone. He waved it off and activated his GlobeX Sat/Sync 800. He listened intently, his left hand over his left ear to screen out the plane noise. A few curt replies ended the call.

"Traveling under the name of Hudson, so if she checks in anywhere it will probably be that name also," said Lucas.

"How do you know if it's New York or New Jersey, or God knows where?" asked Devon.

"Montez landed in La Guardia; it's the city, for sure. The police there have it all networked. We'll find her."

Fifteen minutes later the stewardess came back. "Another call," she said, "we transferred it to you."

It was from the New York police. "She checked into the Roger Smith Hotel last night. We have a man on his way now."

"Don't arrest her," said Lucas. "She may lead us to the others."

"The net's closing, boys," he said flipping his phone closed.

"This is the third straight holiday season I've been working," said Lucas.

"Yeah, my wife's not thrilled about it either," said King.

"Can't this wait until Monday, mine said," piped in Devon.

"I think it will be over before Monday," said Lucas.

They looked over at Larry. He was playing Creature Hockey on his laptop.

23

Friday Noon

Lucas, King, Devon, and Larry landed at 10:42 A.M. They caught a cab to the Roger Smith and let King pay. Detective Finley was waiting, from Manhattan-South.

"All the guys from the Times Square precinct are busy with the New World preparations," he said.

The desk clerk at the Roger Smith looked at the picture of Elaine.

"I think she left an hour ago. Didn't ask us for any directions. Didn't look like a reveler either. She had a small backpack. Looked very determined. There was another woman with her."

Lucas pulled out the photo of Maria.

"Yeah, that's her."

"So, we have the link," he said.

"Shit, now what?" said Devon.

"I'll circulate the photos with the police, but they expect a million people here tonight. Just crowd control will keep them busy until morning," said Finley.

"What do we do if the trail gets cold?" asked Devon.

"Hope."

Larry and Devon left to scan the area. Larry had a MacHand rigged with a directional antenna mounted so that he could pick up Elaine's signals within a one-mile radius. Then he could monitor her transmissions until capture. His cell phone was strapped to his side, with Finley's number in memory 1. They walked west on 50th Street, the tall buildings blocking and reflecting signals in the narrow streets. Triangulating her signal would be difficult. He tried to minimize these problems by rotating the antenna. He had no way to correct for the millions of cell signals bouncing off the walls. Even if they had her number it would take minutes to trace her location. If she hung up, they'd have to search further.

Devon asked, "Don't all these things have GPS accuracy down to a yard or so?"

"Yep, since 2010," said Larry.

"Then why can't we trace her faster and better?"

"She's disabled it in all her devices."

"I thought that was impossible without destroying the machine?"

Larry raised an eyebrow and shook his head. "She's at the envelope. We're not chasing Little Miss Riding Hood here."

Elaine had just finished her mini-test and was eating lunch from the sack she had brought. Cheese, pretzels, Snapple, and a Mars bar. Miranda wasn't much company, so Elaine took the cushions off the couch and lay down for a nap.

Larry typed a message to Elaine, "Excalibur to Circuit Chief," it started. "How are my babies doing?"

"I thought her e-mail was closed?" said Devon.

"I used my rendition of Gate Crasher. Now that I have her signature, I may be able to entice her to break silence and answer me. I routed it through Pittsburgh."

Finding the Montezes was proving harder. Although the reservation was in Sal's name, John had moved it to his credit card to get mileage points. He also hoped he could pay the bill before Sal noticed. The police were left with photos taken from the search of the Montez home. That meant 164 concierges to check in Manhattan alone. With the holiday crush it took all of King's persuasion and clout to get any detectives assigned to work with him. The footwork involved would be tedious any day, but, with the crowds, guests could walk in and out of any place unnoticed. They needed some luck. They started with the hotels near the Roger Smith.

To complement that, they also started an APB on both women, and their photos were being copied for circulation. That would take several hours.

24

Friday Afternoon

When lunch was finished Sal suggested they go to Bloomingdale's, "for the ladies."

"We'd love to Dad, but John is taking me to the museums. Want to come?"

"Us? You know how I hate museums, get those 'museum legs', and your mother can' walk that much."

"Because she's fat," murmured Maria.

Rosa was too focused on John and how nice he was to notice. "You kids enjoy. Just be back at the hotel by seven."

John put Sal and Rosa into a cab, then turned to Maria. "You could have the courtesy to ask first."

"I'm playing this one by the seat of my pants."

"How unlike you. What happened to 'Miss Plan Ahead'?"

"She'll be back tomorrow."

"Changed, I hope."

Maria kissed John on the cheek, counter currents of emotion surging back and forth. He hailed the next cab, cut Maria a perturbed look, and headed off on his own. Ariel stepped out from under the restaurant canopy and filled Maria in.

"She is the final link," said Ariel.

"And where do I meet her?" asked Maria.

"In the graveyard at Trinity Church. You can talk freely there."

The next cab refused the fare, "It's murder down there, too much traffic."

Maria walked up 57th Street to 5th Avenue, and then down the steps to the BMT. Everyone she passed was in a festive mood, shouting greetings, blowing horns. She even got a "Happy New World" from the man in the token booth. A guy tried to sell her a 5th World t-shirt.

Ariel appeared again on the platform.

"Trying to save a token?" asked Maria.

They got on the first N train heading south. It was crowded with people taking off early from work. Michael stood next to them.

"You must shun her now," he said.

"Ignore the demon," said Ariel. "He leads to sin and perdition."

"Choose," said Michael. "It is not too late."

A rider bumped into Michael. The spirit looked at him, eyes unblinking.

"Sorry, pal," the man said. "Let me make it up to you." He tried to hand Michael a bottle.

"He's not interested," said Maria.

"Come on, it's party time in New York."

"He doesn't drink."

"Doesn't talk either," said the man. "Except for that 'you must shun her' crap. You guys actors?"

"Something like that," said Maria. Neither angel wanted to converse with anyone but her.

The man turned fully and put his arm around Michael. "Loosen up, fella. Two beautiful women, what more do you want? I'm goin' home to the Bell Witch. That's why I drink."

Michael ignored him.

Ariel said, "Maria, we should get off this railway and pick another."

"Railway?" the man said. "This is a subway for Christsake. Railways have locomotives. You must be out-of-towners."

"Yes," said Maria.

"That explains the funny talk. Look, you need directions? I can give you directions."

"Next stop, 34th Street. Please watch the doors," announced the PA system.

"I will follow," said Michael.

Ariel let the doors open and close.

A woman playing a sax, dark glasses over alert eyes, approached. She jingled her cup at the three. "I'm Saxy, how about a contribution?"

Maria dropped in a dollar.

"What would you like to hear?" Saxy said to Michael.

Maria interrupted, "I don't know, how about Silent Night?"

"That's a Christmas song, Toots. Try this." The woman wailed *Auld Lang Syne*. That was more suitable for the turning anyway.

"Fine," said Maria. "Could you play it elsewhere?"

"Freaks," said Saxy, moving along. Ariel touched Maria's shoulder, the first contact they had ever had except in the other realm. Then her hand flew back and hit the glass in the door.

"Here?" Ariel said. "You choose to do battle here?"

Michael was shoved against a pole. He looked at the female angel and snapped his chin. Ariel was thrown up against the corner of the car.

"Give us a break," someone said. "Take your fight elsewhere."

Suddenly Michael landed on the floor and skidded through the crowd backwards.

"Start your party at your own place!" a woman shouted. "I'm trying to read."

The angels were now at opposite ends of the car. Michael rose above the heads of the passengers and flew toward Ariel.

"I thought he didn't drink," said the first man.

The two angels circled each other, backs against the ceiling. A young girl screamed; her mother comforted her. "I've seen worse."

Then the doors sprung open and Ariel blew out, bouncing off the tunnel wall and falling below the wheels. The doors slammed shut. Michael came down and started toward Maria. Ariel appeared again, forced the doors open, and planted her feet on the floor of the car. She sucked in air and blew a blast at Michael, who was thrown against a seat.

"Someone call a cop," said the woman whose lap Michael landed in.

"Canal Street," said the overhead speaker.

They got off.

"You know it is not allowed," said Ariel.

"You should not have touched a human," Michael said.

"You wrestled with Jacob."

"In former times."

"Why don't you both leave?" said Maria. And they did.

Maria sat on the bench, wondering what to do. She boarded the next train and took it to Rector Street.

The graveyard was empty except for a figure sitting near the tomb of Alexander Hamilton. She stood up when Maria approached.

"I'm Betsy," she said, holding out her hand.

Maria shook it and replied, "All I know is I'm to meet someone here. I have no idea why."

"Who sent you?"

"Ariel."

"That's the magic word." She took a small cylinder out of her pocket and handed it to Maria.

"Place that on the end of your videocam tonight. It's a CCD image enhancer, works in light as low as a hundredth of a lux."

"That's almost total darkness."

"I'm an astronomer. Ariel said you might be filming under those conditions."

"Won't you be with us?"

"No. I don't know what you're up to, except that it's God's work. I've been waiting for this my whole life. We knew the date of the beginning of the end was 1914, but we didn't know the day of the battle."

"You're a Witness?"

"Yes, our headquarters are just over there." She pointed to the other end of the Brooklyn Bridge. "All of us wish you well and know that, with Ariel's help, the new world will be the promised reward."

"Don't you want to see our setup?"

"No. We are assembling, all over the world, to pray for the next nine hours. We want to enter Paradise cleansed of our sins."

Then she started to leave.

"Wait. Please," said Maria. "Have you seen an angel called Michael?"

"Yes. He works for the Evil One. We have rejected him."

"I knew I was right," said Maria, then added, "And Miranda?"

"Who's Miranda?"

"I'm just checking everyone."

"God will not let you fail. Be sure of that."

The woman left the graveyard with a little wave to Maria, who looked beyond her down Wall Street. "And the world thinks it turns on this place," she thought.

She walked over to a Sabrett umbrella and bought a hot dog. The stand owner was bundled against the weather.

"Now, you have a nice day," he said.

Rosa was pacing the living room. "Where's John?"

"You know how he is in museums. Never enough. He'll be back shortly," said Maria.

"You could have waited for him."

"Mom, we're grownups, we can be apart for a little while."

"Your father always waits for me."

The apartment bell rang; Maria let John in.

"Forgot to plan our reentry?" he chided.

"They're okay," she whispered. "Getting ready for the big blowout."

25

The Eve of the 5th World

For 354 days it waited, perched 120 feet atop the silver pole, looking down on Times Square. Unlike in previous years it was turned on every evening in December, counting the nights until the New Age. This night The 5th World Ball would attract the eyes of 8 billion people as it slid slowly down to its resting place.

At 6 P.M. the ball turned on. Its 10-foot diameter burst with illumination as 720 halogen lamps and 288 xenon glitter strobes shot light beams through the ventilation holes and off the 24,000 silver rhinestone reflectors that covered the outer surface. Eight 10,000 watt xenon lamps inside the ball projected brilliant rays into the air. The clear winter evening augmented the view. A fog machine created enough mist to scatter the radiation and show the paths of the beams.

Then a display began from the other buildings. Powerful lasers and search lights covered the sky with tracers of silver and white, forming a series of canopies over the crowded square. Sometimes they reflected off the people below who waved Mylar pompons in the air. The cone-shaped shafts bounced off windows or rose unreflected into the black sky, pulse rates carefully monitored to prevent seizures among epileptics in the crowd.

It was dark now and Larry was getting a faint signal. "Hello, wizard. You do good work," it said. She was logging on somewhere close.

Larry answered, "The best. Hope you found it useful."

To Devon he said, "I need a more direct path. The multiple reflections are increasing the noise ratio."

Devon suggested a rooftop, so they entered the tallest nearby building.

"We don't let anyone on the roof," the building manager said. "Insurance problems."

Devon dialed Finley.

"Okay, if the NYPD says so, it's yours. But sign this first," said the manager. He handed them an insurance waiver.

The 56-story building had a roof whose view was blocked to the west by Rockefeller Center and to the north and east by other buildings.

"That's all right," said Larry, "the signal is coming in strong from over there." He pointed south, toward Times Square.

"What's it saying?"

"She's accessing her e-mail again, transmitting to us."

"You'll have to show me the blueprints. I did a cobble job to shunt your detours aside," sent Elaine.

Larry said, "...wait, she's off...Damn it. She's gone."

"How far away was she?"

"Less than half a mile as the crow flies."

They looked at their overview map of Manhattan. Larry circled a three-block radius, centered on 42nd and Broadway.

"Ninety percent chance she's inside there," Larry said.

"Let's get closer," said Devon.

"Let me deposit something in her bin first," said Larry. He typed, "Supposed to be foolproof, but you hacked your way by. Where did you learn the trade?"

Maria came out of her room looking radiant.

"Is that the dress you wore to the University Ball?" asked Rosa.

"Yes, Mother. It still fits."

John walked past and went into the bedroom to finish his dressing.

Rosa sipped a martini; Sal coughed in the bedroom.

"When is he going to get that checked?" asked Maria.

"Never. He thinks it's a flu, a five-year flu. I keep at him, but..."

Sal came into the living room in his tux.

"Dad! You look great."

"If this cummerbund don' strangle me I'll make it. Getting those studs through the collar almost gave me arthritis."

"You have arthritis," said Rosa.

He poured himself a martini.

"You gotta learn to handle these," he said, raising his glass. "They get me through the day."

"Maybe next year, Dad. One thing at a time."

John came out of the bedroom. He wore a tuxedo with a turned-down collar. As usual, he cleaned up well, almost made Maria jealous.

"Pictures!" Sal shouted, and began the ritual of who was to stand next to whom, who was to take the photo, how many of each couple...

"Now, one of you and Mom," said Sal to Maria.

"Use the soft focus," said Rosa.

"Martini, John?" asked Sal.

"Sure."

"Maria, baby, aren' you excited about tonight?" asked Sal, watching his daughter look out the window.

"Very, Dad. I'm thinking of all that's happened during the thousands of years that led up to this."

"Let's not get too deep. It's a night for fun."

"She's back on," Larry said. "Strong signal, I can trace this one."

Devon and Larry went down the elevator, hoping any signal wouldn't be blocked by the metal cage. She came on again when they entered the lobby.

"Now we follow, like crumbs on a forest trail," said Larry.

They turned left, walked over to Sixth Avenue, then left again to 48th Street. Elaine was off again; they stopped.

"Not a problem now, her footprint signal narrowed the area. I can get close," said Larry.

"We gotta' get better than close," said Devon.

The two couples walked into the lobby and waited for a taxi.

"I'll get you as close as I can," said the driver. "But you may have a little walk."

It wasn't traffic that slowed them down, it was people. You would have made better time crossing Calcutta during the Vishnu Festival than trying to negotiate crosstown between 30th and 58th Streets. The driver could get no further than 51st Street, between Fifth Avenue and Avenue of the Americas, two blocks from Rockefeller Center. They paid the driver, got out, and walked along Fifth Avenue, in front of the bronze statue of Atlas holding up the world, his knee bent in genuflection aligned perfectly with the tabernacle on the altar of Saint Patrick's Cathedral. There the faithful were already vying for seats for the New World Midnight Mass.

They crossed 50th Street and turned right in the middle of the block across from Saks Fifth Avenue. The view dazzled them. All along the Promenade that led to the Plaza were people in formal dress and trees full of faint white lights. Many jockeyed for railing spots to view the ice skaters on the rink below. Above the rink the golden statue of Prometheus lay sideways, the gift of fire held high in his right hand. Even Maria was overwhelmed.

They walked left, around the rink, to the NBC Today Studio, and then right the half block to the entrance to 30 Rockefeller Plaza. John held the door for them and they entered the famous lobby. Maria looked up at the huge murals of laborers working on colossal projects that filled the ceiling. She thought it appropriate for the evening's plans.

Down the marbled walkway they turned into the fifth bank of elevators, showed the guard their tickets, and took the express marked "Rainbow Room." A 41 second non-stop ride to the 65th floor. They stepped into the maroon and grey hall with its translucent glass, ebony and mahogany columns, and black mirrors to the left that made the columns seem endless. Then they turned right to the reception desk framed by the Empire State building behind; no matter how they had looked to themselves before, everyone now felt handsome or beautiful and sophisticated. They checked their coats, turned left, and walked to the maître D'.

Larry and Devon were standing at 48th and 6th Avenue.

"She's answering again," Larry said.

"No plans tonight in Pittsburgh?" she asked.

"Good," said Devon. "She's getting personal. Keep her going."

Larry typed in, "I'm on my own, as usual. What's happening with you?"

"Ask to see her," said Devon.

"I'm supposed to be in Pittsburgh," said Larry. "And she'd cut me off if I tried. Let me handle this my way. I bet I know what she likes. She's like me."

"I have a little party here," she signaled. "But I can talk later. Should be home tomorrow."

"Christ, tell her anything," pleaded Devon.

"Hey, not so fast," typed Larry. "Tell me what my babies are up to."

"God's work," she replied.

"A religious fanatic, the worst kind," said Devon.

Larry turned so Devon couldn't see the screen. "Can I help?" he asked.

"Gotta' go," she said. "Maybe later."

The Rainbow Room was bursting with people. City lights glinted off the two-story windows, adding a soft glow to the Italian dark purple-brown aubergine silk that covered the walls. The 1930's Art Deco-Moderne room was warm and sensual, elegant and comfortably rich. Dark mirrors gave it an other-worldly feeling. Every table had as many chairs as could fit. The Montezes were placed at one the size of the trays used to bake a New York pizza. How the dinner plates would fit was anyone's guess.

Maria counted the people, well over 300. The fire marshal's sign read, "Occupancy by more than 260 people is dangerous and unlawful." She wondered if that included waiters and staff.

The Montez table was off to the right of the entrance, hidden by the Captain's Bar, not to be seen by the crowds passing by. Behind them the view was to the south, the

Empire State Building illuminated in red, white and blue, the New Freedom Tower that replaced the old World Trade Center Buildings farther off in gold and silver. On the left were the three bridges (Brooklyn, Manhattan, Williamsburg - the BMWs) that connected the island to Brooklyn, each like a necklace of lights across the East River; and, on the right, the Statue of Liberty in soft green.

"Well," said Sal. "We got the view but for $1,500 a pop you expec' more."

"The best seats are near the dance floor," said Rosa.

"It was the luck of the draw," said Sal.

"I saw men passin' hundreds to the maitre d'," said Rosa.

"This is New York," said John.

Maria hadn't spoken.

"Wha'za matter, little girl?" said Sal. "Awestruck?"

"It's overwhelming," she said.

Sal's smile was cut off by an elbow to the ribs.

"There's Colin Powell. He's a New Yorker you know. And that's Mel Gibson," Rosa said pointing with her eyes to the door.

"He did that Mayan movie a few years ago?"

"Yeah, he's really into this stuff."

"And over there..." Rosa continued her recital.

It was already 9 P.M., and the temperature had dropped into the thirties.

"Fuckin' Feds," said Cooley. "The family's having a blow tonight at my sister's and I'm here doing show and tell."

"Yeah," said Fusco. "We're supposed to report to a Neil King, a big badge from DC. Or is that Kneel, King?"

The concierge at the Doral shook her head. They went over to the Benjamin.

The woman at the desk had a thick Arab accent. "Yes, I've seen them. Parents with their daughter and her husband in 2203. Want me to call?"

"No, thanks."

Cooley flipped his phone open and dialed. "King?"

"Yes, this is Agent King."

"Well, *Agent* King, we have your marks."

"Damn," said Lucas. "Their hotel is just around the corner." They were there in 90 seconds.

The small elevator (there were only two) had cameras in the ceiling. Lucas thought someone could check the tapes later. They got off at 22. Four suites filled the floor. 2203 was the two-bedroom to the left when they exited the elevator. The door had a bell mounted on the front.

No answer.

"Call down to the desk and have them send someone up."

The bellman arrived with the key, muttering about intruding on nice people. "The old guy tipped me a sawbuck, why don't you leave them alone?"

The door swung open into a dining room. A small kitchen was to the right, a large living room to the left. The whole place was done in modern Chinese. Both men pulled out their guns.

"I'm gone," said the bellman.

On either side of the living room wall was a door to a bedroom. Lucas took the right. Nothing but old people's clothes. Even the large patio outside the French doors was empty.

King came out the other door. "They're here all right. The girl was in this room."

"Parents in the one I searched."

"Looks like someone has the couch."

"And we're left holding the bag."

Back in the lobby they questioned everyone. The doorman remembered calling them a cab. "About 8 o'clock."

"Where did they go?"

"East, it's a one-way street."

"I mean final destination."

"Didn't ask, didn't say."

"Maybe we can find the cab," said King.

"Ha! Good luck finding anything tonight," the doorman rolled his eyes.

"And you, Madam?" said the waiter to Maria.

She snapped to. "Yes?"

"Dinner orders," said Sal.

"Oh, I'll have the Tournedos Rossini."

"Just look at these plates," said Rosa. "Purple, white, yellow, black, who would have thought they went together? And the design! My."

The band started with "We'll Meet Again."

Sal and Rosa got up. John looked at Maria, "I'd ask you to dance..."

"Not just yet," said Maria, looking past his shoulder at Ariel, standing near the entrance.

The angel nodded. Everything was set.

"Dance?" said Maria. "Yes, of course." She squeezed her chair away from the table, hitting the back of the woman behind her.

"Excuse me," she said.

"No sweat," said the woman. "We'll be banging into each other all night. Skip the apologies."

Maria didn't know if she preferred the frankness to civility. And would either matter in a few hours?

They walked past the other tables and stepped onto the circular revolving dance floor. Maria hadn't been in John's arms for years. Anyone's arms, really. It felt comfortable. She wished she could enjoy it more, but she couldn't focus on the music. John, always a good lead, maneuvered her around the 100-foot circumference, coming up on the Montezes. Rosa rotated Sal so she could watch the couple.

"Easy on my back," said Sal. "I don' want to sit out any of this evening."

"We're not going to hear about your back tonight, are we?"

Maria smiled at her parents, trying to look content. John's artist eyes scanned the room, noting the silver lame tablecloths, the diamond-shaped crystal chandelier ("Sophie Tucker's earring," to regulars), the terraced dining areas. Maria wondered what the rotation rate of the floor was.

"That girl's mind is elsewhere," said Sal. "Why can' she relax anymore?"

It was 11:10. Elaine tossed the copy of Computer World back onto the desk. She wanted to talk to someone and Miranda wasn't it. She turned her portable on and answered Excalibur.

"I'm bored," she began. "Time to kill. Tell me about yourself."

Larry put his MacHand on top of a garbage can lid at 46th and 6th, and answered. "Not much to look at. I stay in the lab all day."

"You know that's not important. How did you construct the chip?"

"From the base up. I had free rein. Everybody's dream."

He moved along the street, eyes glued to the screen, Devon trying to clear a path ahead of him.

"How did you jump my keeper?" she asked.

"I have my own key. How did you wire my processor?"

"Not easy. In fact, very difficult. I sure loved its look."

"You should see it when it's cooking."

"I have. It smokes."

Jesus! She did get it to work!!!!!!!!!

"What will you use them for?"

"No fair asking, just yet. You'll get 'em back."

A reveler bumped Larry and his MacHand crashed to the street. He dove down, shielding it with his body. Devon helped him up.

"You okay?" Devon asked.

"The hell with me. See if this still works." He turned it back on and the screen lit up again. He straightened the antenna and said, "South. She's south of here. Maybe a few blocks."

The band swung into a Lindy, Pennsylvania 6-5000, the 300 multi-colored lights in the dome above, that gave the room its name, glowing and dimming in synchrony with the music.

Maria asked to sit this one out. Her knees were weak from anxiety.

"What I wouldn't give for a hand of bridge," she said.

"Now? Maybe some poker tomorrow in the hotel. You know Sal and his penny-ante," said John.

"I'm just free-thinking. Ignore me."

"Easy to do. Easy to do."

She looked at him, hatred in her eyes, remembering why she had left him in the first place. John got up to find a waiter for drinks. None had cruised by in 40 minutes.

Where Broadway intersected with 7th Avenue, they had her again.

"She's so close I can monitor her every keystroke."

Devon called Finley.

"We'll probably have to walk; the crowds are too thick," said King.

"It's not far," said Finley. "We'll meet them near 44th and Broadway."

Larry and Devon stayed at the corner, even though they were pushed this way and that by people celebrating.

"How's the weather in Pittsburgh?" Elaine asked.

"What do I care? I'm not going out," answered Larry.

"I wish I was back home, too. I get edgy in the 3-D world."

"So do I. I like talking to you this way."

Devon watched Larry's screen. "Can't you ask her where she is?"

"Direct questions spook us," said Larry. "Let me handle this."

Then to Elaine, "I'll pass this party day like I always do, at my monitor."

"Great," she replied. "We'll be together. There's a real doozy of a show coming on in 37 minutes."

Devon looked up at the big digital clock above Times Square. "Shit, that's the stroke of midnight."

"What channel?" Larry asked Elaine.

"We'll access you," she said.

"So, I just keep my terminal on?"

"Doesn't matter. You just watch the screen."

"Is that possible?" asked Devon.

"Yesterday, no. Tonight, apparently so."

"She's going to be on TV in Pittsburgh?"

"Sounds like it. Other places too, I bet."

"Then why does she need to be in New York?"

Lucas, King, and Finley plowed down side streets until they hit 7th Avenue, then headed south to the intersection. People shouted insults at them when they rudely shoved them aside. It took a full five minutes to search the corner and find Larry.

The five men talked over the din of the crowd.

"Real close, real close," said Larry.

"I was afraid of this. They're targeting Times Square," said King.

"And a lot more," said Larry.

Maria watched the New World Clock that had been specifically placed in the Rainbow Room for this evening. She was trying to keep her mind on the project yet look relaxed. Ariel had warned her to act normal. Normal! That was asking too much.

"I haven' been this excited in years," said Sal. "Maybe not ever."

Things were getting noisy. Party hats were falling off, clackers were swung around, horns blared above the sound of the band, and people were popping balloons. Everyone was happy.

The crowd seemed to have doubled every time Maria and John got to the dance floor. Now they switched with their parents, Sal holding Maria.

"Have you been happy, Dad?" she asked.

"With a few hitches it's not been so bad."

"So bad? Didn't you ever want more?"

"I had more than most, that's enough. Your mother and I fight a little, but, all in all we made a decent life."

"I think I want too much."

"The curse of your generation."

Sal escorted Maria through the throng. No one was dancing now, just trying to stay upright and not plow into anyone else. People, sophisticated an hour ago, were bawdy, tripping over one another, laughing at anything.

Hugh Jackman and a cast of Broadway stars tried to sing over the din. They were past the show tunes and on to old favorites. There'd be no more breaks before the New

Age. "New York, New York" rose above the noise. The music was choreographed to keep changing until at midnight it would sound exactly like the Seekers singing "There's a New World somewhere they call the Promised Land..."

26

On TVs all over America, stations vied for viewers. TNN, The Nashville Network, had "Country Welcomes the Next Age" from The Grand Old Opry, starring Tim McGraw and Faith Hill dressed as Mayan singers; Fox was running "New World from Vegas" with stars from the Cirque du Soleil show "Maya"; Gavin McLeod was hosting "New Age Eve with the Royal Canadians, a Salute to Guy Lombardo," on PBS. The Metropolitan Museum had built a Mayan temple on the front steps and Mayan priests re-enacted a sacrificial ritual. A huge screen displayed the Mayan Calendar Clock built in Times Square with its three wheeled cycles as it counted down to the New World. But most sets were turned to 83-year-old Dick Clark (braces hidden in his suit to prop him up) on ABC, set on a wooden stage above the Armed Forces Recruiting Center on 43rd Street, directly below the Times Square Building. His "5th World Rockin' Eve - The Turning of the Cycle - Direct from Times Square," was showcasing all the great hits from the past 60 years. Mayan dancers and singers covered the stage, trying to keep beat with the rock music. That show was hooked in live to Hollywood and another cast of hundreds.

Clark turned away from the camera and surveyed the scene below.

"Hard to believe I'll have to be 5,400 to make the next one," he shouted.

Every time Clark raised his hand, tens of thousands hooted up to the cameras.

"Nothing like this ever," he said. "People as far as I can see, all celebrating. Hope you folks at home can hear me."

"They're celebrating there, too," said co-host Alex Trebek.

Concert JBL speakers blared music into the streets, the revelers dancing out of step, hugging strangers. A drunk was trying to get one of the mounted police Sullivan horses to drink from his cup. The cop chased him away. People linked arms and started a Greek dance, swaying left and right, kicking their legs out; others formed long conga lines and snaked among the throng. The sober stamped their feet and blew into their hands to keep warm. Everyone else was toasty.

"Can you believe this?" asked Clark. "More people having more fun in one place, than ever before in history?"

"Gotta' go with that," said Alex.

ABC broke for commercial.

At 11:35, Maria excused herself from the table and mounted the steps Fred Astaire and Ginger Rogers had danced up so long ago. That brought her above the dance floor in front of a cast-glass wall that glowed softly from behind. For a few seconds she watched her parents dancing, then glanced over at John sitting alone, looking out at the view. After a long minute she walked down the other side and entered the lobby. She turned, went to the ladies' room, looked at herself in the round lighted mirror above the fluted sink, drew in her breath, went down a flight of carpeted steps, and entered the small hall near the grill. Ariel had unlocked the door to the roof. Maria entered the narrow stairwell and climbed out the window. That brought her to the ornate parapet. She stood there and waited.

Over in the bar, the Norman Bel Geddes blimp-like red and black streamlined ocean liner floating above, patrons were toasting the City.

"Hey," said Bill. "Am I seeing right? Is that a woman on the ledge out there?"

His pal turned to look. "Sure as hell is! What's she doing?"

"She's gonna jump," Bill shouted.

Several others looked, too. There was Maria looking up, reaching with her arms. Then she stepped off the roof. But she didn't fall; she flew, off to the southwest.

Bill dropped his glass; the others gaped; one woman screamed.

Now the whole crowd faced the windows. But Maria was gone. Once out of the building lights, she vanished.

"I swear," said Bill. "There was a woman and she jumped."

Several others nodded.

"I think they've been over-juiced," said someone.

The rest of the crowd laughed.

"We all saw it, didn't we?" said Bill.

"I don't know what I saw," said another.

"Ah, the glare from the windows projected something going on inside the building," weezed a drunk.

"Look, you've all had a few," said the bartender. "It's almost midnight; you don't want to miss the Ball coming down."

"Can't you tell us exactly where she is?" shouted King.

"Not in this mess," said Larry. "It's within a few hundred yards, and coming from that direction." He pointed south. "But I'm having trouble getting a zenith angle with all the interference pouring in." He pointed to a huge electric sign.

"I wish I could join you," he typed to Elaine.

"We are joined," she said. "Why ask for anything more?"

"Tell me what you're looking at, besides your screen, and I'll tell you what I'm looking at."

"Sorry, I have a job to do now. Catch you later."

"She's off again, and I don't think she'll be back on before it's over," he said.

"Shit, shit, shit! We almost had her," said Finley.

The guard and technician on the roof of the Times Square Building were re-checking the equipment for the midnight show when the three figures approached. Apparently some revelers had slipped through security.

"Hold it right there," the guard said, his hand raised. "No one's allowed up here but us."

The figures kept coming.

The guard pulled out his pistol. "I mean it. Stop!"

The figures parted: one headed toward the technician, another toward the tower, the third walked straight at the guard.

"I warned you," the guard said, and fired a shot at approaching figure's legs. It kept coming.

He aimed the next bullet at the chest. He must have missed because the figure now grabbed him by the shoulders.

At first the guard resisted, twisting his frame to break the hold. Then he was lifted off his feet, rising with the being that had him in its grasp. They flew over the rail and stopped. The guard was released, and fell five stories to a balcony below. He lay broken on the tiles.

The technician screamed. His attacker had him by the wrist and was twirling him in the air. The figure let go and the man sailed out over the building, bounced off the first balcony, and landed on a patio 13 floors below.

The figures scanned the roof, then left.

A moment later, Ariel and Maria alighted on the roof.

"Where are the guards?" asked Maria.

"Yes, they should be here," said Ariel.

Elaine, clutching the overnight bag, opened the door; Miranda followed and stepped out onto the roof, then stood guard at the door.

"Hail, sister," said Ariel. "You have chosen the correct path."

"Yes. I am with you now," said Miranda.

"The Lord will reward His faithful."

Elaine opened her bag near an outlet.

Maria took out The Savior, inspected it one last time, then unraveled the wire to the base of the tower. She lifted the 4" wide metal collar, with its spring-mounted catch and, with Elaine's help, snapped it to the mast just above the 5th World sign, in the exact spot where the Ball would stop falling and go out at the stroke of midnight. Elaine fastened the collar tightly with a cinch bolt, making sure the contact would hold. She sprayed Scotch Guard over the bottom of the connection to keep moisture out and taped the wire to the post below so there would be no strain on the ring. Maria cleaned any grease off the pole above, did a continuity test to insure that the collar would electrify the Ball, and stepped back to inspect her work. The Ball would make excellent contact. Good. She rattled the mast to see that everything was tight.

Elaine positioned The Savior 20 feet from the tower, three feet from a grounded outlet. She plugged it in, secured the connection with a safety strap, then anchored it to the floor of the roof with three 2" wood screws. Then she went over to the videocam, took off the shroud, plugged the cord into the other outlet, fitted the CCD detector between the lens and the body, and checked to see that the shutter was open. She scanned the rooftop, taking in Maria, the roof's edge, the lights from below. Miranda wasn't registering.

Not one to question, Elaine brought her eye away from the rubber cup and looked at the other angel. Ariel nodded. All that was left was the wait.

From below, the noise of the crowd began to increase.

On the stage at the foot of the building, Dick Clark was speaking into a microphone.

"Nine minutes to midnight," he said. "Then, not just a new year, not just a new century, but a New World!"

The rock band swung into more traditional tunes and studio lights reflected off a turning glass ball suspended from a cherry-picker.

The dance floor in the Rainbow Room was turning, too, purple, gold, green and silver light ovals bouncing off the dome and across the faces of the dancers. All the Fellini-like party hats were on except for Maria's, which lay on the table in front of her chair. Saxophones took over the melody, as if to slide everyone into the next age.

"You two get back on the floor," said John to Maria's parents. "We'll join you as soon as she gets back. If there's room." Then he headed for the entrance, hoping to catch a glimpse of Maria in the crowd.

The hallways were as full as the dance floor, people sloshing their drinks on one another; singles herded in a corner near the bar. Maria wasn't to be found, so John went back to the dining room, in the hope he had passed her on the way out. She'd promised that tomorrow would be better, that she would explain all of her behavior. But it wasn't tomorrow yet.

At 11:40, Finley put his hand over his left ear to shut out the crowd and asked the caller to repeat the message.

"Got it," he said, then cupped his hand over his mouth and shouted into Lucas's ear, "Masters been sighted, follow me."

The five men wove their way over to 42nd Street and found the kiosk.

"Yeah, they just handed me the photo to hang up. I seen her around noon. Gimme six crumbled up bills for a computer mag."

"Where did she go?" asked King.

"The reward," the man shouted. "The reward." Pointing to the poster.

"That comes later," said King. "Tell us where she is now."

"No way. I want my money now."

"Do you know the penalty for hindering an arrest?"

"What's she done?"

"We don't know yet, but I'm acting on the highest authority," King said, flipping his badge at the man.

"Who the fuck cares who you are? I want the money first."

Finley took over. "Look, pal, you'll get your money, but we need to know now!"

"Ten percent, I want 10% minimum, now."

"What's that?"

"Five Ben Franklins. I'm a clam 'til I see green."

King, Lucas, Devon, and Finley stood in a circle collecting the $500. Finley shoved it at the man. "We don't see her, I'll be back."

"There, she went in there," said the man, pointing to One Times Square. "Anodda lady was with her, but I tink I seen 'em leave later."

"She's back on," said Larry. "And it's with the Excalibur! No transmission yet, but she's plugged in, up and running."

They hurried over to the building's entrance. The guard waved his hands and shouted, "Go away, the building's closed."

They put their badges up against the glass. "You open this fuckin' door, or you'll be in The Tombs before daybreak," said Finley.

When they got inside they asked for the visitor's log. Everyone who'd checked in that day had also signed out. Had they come and gone?

"Strong signal," said Larry. "She's here, this is the place."

"Can you tell us where in the building it's coming from?" asked King.

"Upstairs. Way up. I'll know when I get closer."

They took the elevator to the top floor.

"Still higher," said Larry.

"The roof," said Finley. "Where the ball comes down!"

27

11:54 P.M.

Ariel, Maria, and Elaine stood near The Savior, staring at the digital clock mounted on the roof. It read "11:54:17."

"Hear me!" a voice shouted behind them. It was Michael. "Remove your machine."

Maria turned and stepped between Michael and The Savior.

"Him again?" shrieked Elaine.

"Lucifer has returned," said Ariel.

"Don't let him near the equipment," said Maria. "He wants to stop us."

"Why?"

"Because his kind want to control the world."

"The time has come. Your world will end if you do not heed. Reject Satan. Let me help you," said Michael.

"He lies, they all lie. The lie is their God," said Ariel.

Maria whispered to Elaine, telling her that neither the demon nor the angel could touch The Savior. They needed humans for that.

11:56 P.M.

Michael started the first display. He rose off the ground, a light coming from his chest. His clothes fell off, and wings appeared on all sides, beating a wind across the roof. From his mouth issued a golden trumpet, and music filled the rooftop. He played a plaintive melody, the notes clear in the cold air. The crowd below cheered.

Maria almost fainted, so beautiful was the music. She stared at the lovely angel.

"Look away, before he deceives you," said Ariel, who jumped to the top of the guardrail. Then she stretched out her arms and a blue light slowly spread across the entire building until the whole roof glowed. An impressed murmur echoed through the revelers in the street. Her giant wings were of layered gossamer and through them Maria could see the stars, brighter than the city lights, the Belt of Orion shimmering behind the screen.

Maria was overwhelmed. These beings were beyond her scope; she needed time to take in their magnificence, time to analyze it, time to tell right from wrong.

Larry was the first one on the stairwell. Devon helped guide him so that he didn't trip on a step, so concentrated was he on tracing the source. Devon held the super-conducting magnet in his hand away from Larry's MacHand.

"All we need is to get close and that'll wipe out her program," said Larry.

When they turned the first landing, they saw Miranda.

"Who are you?" said Devon.

"A friend."

"She's the one who stole the Excaliburs," said Larry.

"Is the roof open? Where are the guards?" asked Devon.

"Everyone is fine, but you cannot go up there."

"It's stronger," said Larry. "I know she's on the roof.'

"Who?" asked Miranda.

"Elaine Masters. We have to see her."

"She left."

"Without her computer? Not likely."

Miranda was now close to the two men. Devon reached up to push her aside.

"You are not to touch me!"

She jumped back and began to change. First her limbs turned into legs, hair-covered, ending in paws; her neck thickened and her face pulled forward into a snout; her ears moved to the top of her head and her eyes turned yellow. She slid her tongue over her fangs, and moved her cat body down the steps.

"Jesus," Devon said to Larry. "You were right."

"Back away," the cat hissed. "I don't want to harm you."

"You have to let us by," said Devon.

"Never! Our mission transcends your curiosity. Don't become martyrs for a cause you cannot comprehend."

"You're a construction of my imagination," hoped Devon, as he mounted the next three steps.

Miranda curled her front paw; the nails sprung out; she took her first swipe at him. Devon rose up, caught in her grasp, disemboweled, and then tossed in the air. He fell with a thud, half over the railing, and dropped the magnet down the stairwell. Larry backed down the steps, holding his forearm between him and the cat.

"Shut your machine off," hissed Miranda.

"No! I'm gonna' stop you!" said Larry.

"You remember me, Larry?" it said. "I know ways to turn you inside out."

And with that she leapt at the terrified man. Larry tried to keep her from his head by ramming his arm across her mouth. She bit it off, and cast it aside.

Then she looked at him and said, "I have a purpose beyond your understanding. You were foolish to join with them. Now you must die."

Finley and Lucas were almost to the landing when they saw what was happening. Finley drew his gun and got off one shot before the cat disappeared. He looked at the mutilated man, then at the closed door ahead.

"We've got to get him to a doctor," said Lucas.

"Later. I'll tourniquet the arm now. By the time we get a doctor for him we can be on that roof and stop them," said Finley.

Miranda came back onto the roof, calmly watching her two brethren argue.

"How many will you kill this night?" said one.

"Not as many as you kill and damn," said the other.

Miranda signaled to the women to ignore the angels and proceed with their work.

"God is ready for you to finish," she said.

11:58 P.M.

The door to the roof was welded shut with two inches of thick steel, framed in four-inch molding. Finley banged on it with both fists.

"Police! Open up!"

"Ignore them, Maria," said Miranda. "Intruders cannot but harm our purpose."

They pounded harder, then Finley put his ear to the door and said, "I can't make out what they're saying."

"There should be two guards out there, too," he said.

"Whoever you are, open this door! Don't make it harder on yourself," screamed Finley.

Miranda walked over to Ariel. "Satan has them in his power. I have the door secure."

"Your help will be written in the ledger."

"Can you keep them out?" asked Maria.

"Be assured," said Miranda. "They will not hinder you."

"Damn, it will take half an hour in this mess to get a man up here who can open this," said Finley.

The three men ran back down to the 22nd floor and took the elevator to the lobby. Finley phoned for a doctor for Larry.

28

Do you reject Satan?

11:59 P.M.
One minute to the 5th World

At precisely 11:59, the Mayor of New York hit the red button on the remote, and the winch motor mounted on the roof let out the 1/2" steel cables that held the 1000 pound ball; it began to descend.

As bright as the ball had been for the last hours, it now came alive and beamed far brighter. The lamps inside the sphere began a full rotation every second, causing the ball to appear to pulse in exact time with the digital clock. The computer-driven timer was in phase lock with the National Institute for Standards and Technology in Gaithersburg,

Maryland, as precise as atomic science could measure. The external strobes began to flash in unison. The million people in the street and the billions watching on TV started to shout. The huge three wheeled Mayan calendar above the stage ticked one cog at a time as it neared the end of the 4th World, in perfect sync with the NIST clock..

Dick Clark spoke into the camera, "Just one more minute, folks. Now 55 seconds to a New World."

"You must choose now," said Michael. "The world awaits."

"You have chosen," said Ariel. "Do not let the Beast turn you away from the work of God."

"The Devil knew your weakness was pride - thinking you could control people's destiny. You love power. That is why he chose you. Think of your arrogance, calling your creation 'The Savior,'" said Michael.

"I wish I could be sure," said Maria. "Help me, Elaine."

Elaine was cowering in the corner, the spectacle around her more than anything she could have imagined, even in the deepest hallucinations of her college days. She tried to speak, but all that came out was a soft, "Ariel, Ariel."

"It is your decision alone," said Michael. "Reject the false God. Send him back, chained, to his pit. Know that good triumphs."

"You have the Scriptures to guide you: 'In the Face of Evil, God's Will Be Done'," Ariel said.

Maria moved behind the beautiful woman, for protection from Michael.

11:59:15

"Remove the collar!" bellowed Michael.

"I am not afraid of you," Maria whimpered. "You would have harmed me already if you could."

"Fear him not," said Ariel, spreading a wing around the frightened girl. "I will never let him harm you."

"Maria! Listen to me!" ordered Michael.

11:59:30

Dick Clark was crooning, "Half a minute, guys. I hope you can hear me over the noise."

Searchlights from the streets formed a steeple over the building.

"Act now, or watch your world end," said Michael. "Who are you to decide for others? Have you not sinned? Can you be the example for all?"

Now Maria doubted more than she had before. Could she take the chance, give up control? How was she to know which was the true angel? Michael offered her a way out, relief from her burden, a chance to wash her hands of responsibility. And his majesty frightened her so. Never had anyone intimidated her before. But Ariel was her friend, her protector. Hadn't she saved her from the truck? And wasn't she now protecting her from Michael? And wasn't she needed for this monumental task?

"You tried to kill me with that truck," she said to Michael.

"Their diversion," he replied.

"Get thee gone!" Ariel spat at Michael.

"The Devil damned thee and thy cohorts, vile and evil one!" said Michael.

Elaine squeaked, "The ball is past halfway!"

"How can I choose?" said Maria.

"Think," said Ariel. "You are a brilliant woman. Your reason will prevail."

"Trust not to reason, child," said Michael. "Only through faith will you see."

11:59:40

Maria was lost. Where should she turn? Why had she been chosen? She squatted down below the falling ball, the words of the angels resonating in her ears. Then words of Christ filled her head, "He who humbles himself shall be exalted." She didn't care if she was exalted; she just wanted to do what was right.

She looked up, dropped to her knees, and began to rapidly recite, "Our Father, Who art in Heaven."

11:59:42

"Hallowed be Thy name."

Ariel removed her wing from around Maria and stared at her face.

"Thy kingdom come, Thy Will be done. On Earth as it is in Heaven."

11:59:46

"Give us this day our daily bread, and forgive us our trespasses, as we forgive those who trespass against us."

"No!" shouted Miranda.

11:59:48

"And lead us not into temptation."

Ariel began to move away.

"But deliver us from evil."

A loud crack rent the air; Ariel was thrown back against the railing. Maria looked up at the ball, now more than three quarters of the way down. Beams of light shot from it, bathing Maria and Elaine in crystal brightness, almost blinding them. On its top they saw a magnificent angel, looking directly into their eyes.

It was Michael.

11:59:50

Maria and Elaine raced to the tower. Elaine already had the wrench out and began to unfasten the collar. They shook with fear but managed to snap off the final connection.

"Hurry, hurry," said Maria. "My God, hurry!"

11:59:56

Now, as the xenon lamps blasted their powerful pulses of light through the ball, Maria couldn't see. But the collar came loose and, with a final twist, dropped free, just as the ball touched the contact point, cutting Maria's hand.

"Your Savior bled too when he was lanced on the cross of your salvation," said Michael.

29

Midnight

The 5th World

The New World Ball went out, plunging the roof into darkness. Immediately below the parapet the giant New Age sign clicked on, its 2000 350 watt locomotive headlamps and glitter strobes pulsing the declaration of the 5th World in increasingly larger numerals. Tons of iridescent confetti dropped from the rooftops, turning the night sky into a kaleidoscope. People's shouts and cheers rose from the streets into the air. Maria and Elaine picked themselves up from the deck, the auxiliary lamps kicked in, and they could see again. What they saw was startling.

As programmed, roof-mounted lasers on the Times Square Building, and several other buildings nearby, began to form huge 3-D holograms of historic figures and events, bigger and more fantastic than any Macy's Thanksgiving Day Parade. From the dawn of creation there were Adam and Eve; Pharaohs appeared, their pyramids behind them; Caesar and Christ came next; Mayan priests lifted their arms high above their altars; King Arthur and his Royal Knights galloped past, then Magellan and Columbus. Giant speakers were playing, "There's a new world somewhere, they call the Promised Land…"

But Maria's eye was elsewhere.

Ariel was standing near the corner of the roof, transforming. First its clothes flew off, then its head grew bigger than the ball, and serpents writhed in its hair. Appendages, more like cloaks than wings, sprouted from its back, ribbed to hold the thick covering, fangs at each spine of its ribbing. Its legs ended in claws that gripped the rail around the roof. Its breast was covered with purple eyes. Blood dripped from its neck, and filth issued from its mouth.

And it was male.

"Where you have sowed hope, I will reap death!" he said.

Then he lifted up his arms and cried, "Come, my faithful! Attend me, as we slay these intruders who dare to do battle with us for this world."

His consort Sin appeared, clutching their child Death. Dagon and Chemosh were at her side, escorting the wicked woman to her lover.

Miranda changed into her true form, Beelzebub, the one who is equal to the Devil. Rimmon leaped down from above the tower, and landed within feet of Elaine. Moloch flew over the edge of the roof and hovered near Maria. Arioc showed her ugly face, holding the head of Judas in her hand.

But the Commander of the Heavenly Host came between the terrified women and the demons. Michael, in all his glory, arraigned as he had been in Maria's apartment, stepped in front of her and bellowed, "Ye messengers of war, now is the moment we have awaited! Man has kept his covenant with God, we will defend him."

In answer, the faithful angels appeared, the sound of their beating wings like that of many-horsed chariots rushing into battle. There was Urale, yellow as the sun; Gabriel, flames licking at his body; Raphael, a great seraph - as Satan had been - standing with his staff of burnished silver; Mithra and Zephon blew trumpets to herald the battle.

Then a mighty angel, his feet pillars of fire, came down from Heaven clothed in a cloud. It was Camael, Prince of the Powers, charged with controlling demons, ready to strike the first blow. When he spoke it was like thunder, "We will send you back from whence you came and from which you will not escape." His horde of followers fanned out, encircling the Archfiend.

A black figure stepped forward from the ranks of the good angels. He was Azrael, the Angel of Death, who could kill with a blink of his red eye. He motioned for Camael to begin.

Maria and Elaine clung to each other, not daring to move from the spot where they were rooted.

Satan moved his right arm forward; his warriors attacked.

It was not like any human war. The angels grew to a hundred times a human's size, their beautiful wings now muscled and sinewed. Their weapons were ancient and powerful: great swords, sharp pikes, curved shields. The demons were more frightful. Their limbs were like prehistoric animals, huge and mighty, grasping battering rams, their black amour full of long thick spikes. They moved at will over great distances, the sky their battle theater. The crowds in the street cheered. Elaine saw a huge fiery sword, over two blocks long, slice the night sky and hurl thousands of demons upward. Then, by some unknown force, vile Rimmon was thrown across town, careening off the Empire State Building.

High above, on yellow-black clouds, the Saints watched, seemingly impassive. Moloch, in the grasp of a heavenly cherub, turned this way and that, and screamed for relief. The cherub squeezed harder; green pus oozed out from Moloch's gut. Requel attacked Sin. The two females ricocheted across the sky, neither seeming to gain the advantage. They fell behind the Waldorf-Astoria, out of sight of the roof. Puffs of smoke rose into the sky. Raphael and Beelzebub locked together in a mighty hold, muscles rippled in the silver light, then vaulted into the sky. Up, up they went, above the city of cheer, into the heavens. Maria saw neither again.

Then a hot wind blew from the north, scorching the sides of the building and turning the rails red. Elaine felt the tar on the roof begin to soften. Then Ithuriel waved her hand and cut off the head of the demon Chemosh and the wind abated. A rain of horrible insects came down on the roof. Zephon pursed her lips and blew them away.

The dark forces had their victories too. Urale, smote by a great wind which threw him in the air, landed on the roof of Citicorp. Gabriel, his wounds gushing a gold liquid, fell against the tower, under the weight of Arioc. They wrestled together, rolling across the roof. Abdiel was pinned under the fiend Nisroc, as two demons tore his wings off and pierced his breast with a spear. Baalim cut a wide swath with his lance, throwing dozens of Virtues off the roof. Everywhere there was battle. The crowd along the streets was delirious, shouting, "More, more!"

Camael led his forces against the might of Hell. Maria could see little of the battle, the great figures appearing and disappearing as if the lights were flickering, some of them among the historic laser parade confusing the people who were watching from below. It was impossible to tell who was winning.

The Red Dragon appeared, blaspheming God, its seven heads and ten horns poised toward Michael. The moon became as blood, and scorpions on the dragon's back raised their tails. Michael took a sickle in hand and waited for the dragon to come forward.

But then Heaven opened and a woman appeared holding her Son. The dragon spewed fire at them; it dissipated harmlessly into the sky. People blessed themselves. Then the woman spoke to the dragon. "I have come to absolve the curse of Eve." The beast cowered, unable to resist. The woman stepped forward and placed her foot on its head. Michael cut the head off.

Now everyone, including the supernatural warriors, knew that the main battle was joined. It would be between Michael and Satan.

The great foes circled above the building, ignoring the carnage raging around them. Satan appeared larger than the Archangel, his body lined with rolls of muscles, his eyes fixed on his foe, horns sprouted from his head. Michael waited, his face set in a firm stare. Satan hissed; threw thick flames forward; Michael raised his shield and deflected the heat.

"We meet again, lap-dog," said Satan.

"And again, I will conquer you, false master of the doomed," said Michael.

"Join me now; it is not too late!"

"And live a vile and wretched existence, far from the sight of God?"

The Devil swirled his great tail at the Archangel, curling its tip around Michael's trunk. Michael reached down to pull it away, and Satan caught him a blow that reeled the good angel backwards, still in the hold of the demon.

"He's losing," shouted Elaine.

But Michael struck Satan with a mighty swing of his arm, broke the hold, and hurled the demon away. Then he launched his spear at the huge head, but the Evil One shunted it aside. The crowd hollered, "Yeah!"

"Your ignorance stokes my anger," sneered Satan.

They flew at each other again, their bodies coiled in furious combat, tearing at each other's faces, hands and claws raking, twisted limbs coiled in fight, rage in their eyes. Michael slashed his dagger across the Devil's face, and cut out his left eye. Satan jammed his feet against his foe and tossed him back toward the roof.

Then the Devil leapt upon the rail near the roof's edge, his enemy below him. He lifted the three-ton compressor from the roof, held it above his head and shouted, "Now I have you in my power, weakling!"

Then he hurled the machine downward.

Michael jumped to the side as the compressor buried itself in the roof floor, then he backed toward the tower. He grasped the mast in his hand, tore it from its holding, and, with a cry of "*Imperet tibi Dominus Deus et te vastet!*" [The good Lord will rebuke and plunder you!] charged his archenemy. Michael buried the pole deeply into Satan's chest. It stopped where Satan's body met the ball. The Devil fell forward, gasped and tried to speak, the huge spear through his heart. He squirmed and bellowed, tried to pull the pole out; brimstone poured from his wounds.

"You fool!" he rasped. "We could have ruled the heavens together, sharing the wonder. But you stayed at His side, no more than a servant."

"You were the smartest one, yet you raised a battle you could not win," said Michael. "Think of where you are being cast again. Eternity in chains."

And with that, Michael lifted the Devil above the throng, for all to see his defeat. The crowd chanted, "Nah,

nah, nah, nah, hey, hey, hey, goodbye..."Then, with a shout, he threw the beast down, and Maria could see him falling, falling beyond the streets, beyond the earth, back to his putrid pit, to be chained again in the ice and fire.

The other demons scurried like vermin over the sides of the roof, disappearing before they dropped into the night. The wounds of the good angels healed, severed limbs reattaching, their countenances smoothing back to perfection.

A voice from above said, "Behold, the tabernacle of God is with man. They shall be His people and He their God."

Michael sat down, exhausted, and looked at Maria and Elaine. "You will be a lesson to all. Your names will be read in the Book of Virtue. Your reward great."

"I don't care about that," Maria replied. "My God, I made the right choice." She sat on the roof, dazed, her head in her hands.

The angelic host vanished into the night, leaving nothing to show of the destruction that had occurred. Only Michael remained.

Dick Clark asked Alex Trebek, "Ever see so many people having such a good time?"

"Never, Dick. And what a laser show! Everything went so smoothly."

"That display above the rooftops! The angels! Wow! The crowds loved it!"

"Only in New York."

"We'll be back in a few minutes with the President and the First Husband from the White House," said Clark.

But it wasn't only in New York. The world saw the show, what the cameras could catch of it, and marveled. Reports would vary but most thought it was Hollywood at its best. The few who wrote of a real celestial battle were ignored, even by the New Agers. No – the 5th World was here and it had started with a bang. Hope spread like a golden curtain over the world; love followed. Mankind would have a new chance and things would be better. *How could it be otherwise,* everyone thought?

"Where's the nearest helicopter pad?" asked King.

"There's one over on top of the Seagram's Building on 38th Street," said Finley.

Finley called into headquarters. They would divert a helicopter to the Seagram's pad. Arrival in 14 minutes.

Getting through the crowds was no easy task. Everyone wanted to celebrate, even with the cops. Finley led the wedge, Lucas and King behind. They were on the Seagram's roof at 12:19.

"Take us over to One Times Square," said Finley.

The chopper lifted straight up 30 feet, then leaned and angled the few blocks to where the ball had descended.

Michael touched the two women on the clefts above their lips, lightly, so they would remember some things but not be able to speak of them. Then he lifted them in his arms.

"Can you forgive me?" asked Maria.

"Ours is neither to forgive nor to damn; that is the Lord's. Nor do we harbor memories of human faults. We are the present. When we speak of things gone by, it is God heralding the past through us."

"Please put me down," said Elaine.

"Come with me to celebrate," said Maria.

"I celebrate in my own way," said Elaine, stepping back on the roof.

"Let her be," said Maria.

Michael flew with Maria to the Rainbow Room ledge and placed her gently on the lip.

"Will we see you again?" she asked.

"That is not of my choosing."

"Why do you only come when things are bad?"

"You know not when we come nor when we leave."

Bill, in the bar, saw the whole thing: the same woman coming back, alone, to the ledge. He waved his hand before his face.

"Bullshit," he said, and kept drinking.

Elaine went over to her portable and saw the message.

"On the steps," it read. "Please."

She went to the door, now caved in from the battle, stepped over the twisted metal and looked down. Yes, there was someone in a pool of blood, his right hand on his keyboard. She went down to him, passing the dead body of Devon.

"Excalibur?" she asked.

"Yes," said Larry.

Then she heard the helicopter. "Help is coming," she said and ran back up to the roof.

Elaine went over and disconnected The Savior, placed it carefully in the overnight case, and started disassembling the camera. The searchlight lit up the rooftop, passing over the two dead bodies on the floors below, looking for anyone. The light blinded Elaine. She held her arm over her brow and closed the lid of her portable.

"Stay where you are, Miss Masters!" shouted King. "This is the FBI. Put everything down and place your hands on the top of your head."

Elaine obeyed. Finley and King went down the ladder; Lucas above in the chopper, rifle aimed at Elaine.

They frisked the girl, found nothing, and told her to mount the ladder.

"There is a man on the stairs who needs help," she said.

"We have someone coming over," said Finley.

"Can I stay on the ladder and have you fly me around above the crowd?"

"This isn't funny, young lady," said Finley.

"You have one heck of an explanation ahead of you," said King to the girl.

"Yep."

King looked at Lucas and Finley. What could they charge her with? Roof trespassing? Failure to heed an officer? Who were the two dead bodies? Was Masters involved in the priest's death? Not likely. What about the monster they'd met on the steps - where was she? What was she? What the hell had really happened? Did Masters still have the stolen chips? Would she be prosecuted for that if they were returned unharmed? What would the lawyers say? They'd have to get their shit together before they started explaining this to their superiors.

And where was Montez?

30

The Dawn of the 5th World
December 22, 2012

Maria opened the door to the stairway and saw the long conga line wending its way around the 65th floor. Everyone was singing, "Shake, shake, shake, Honora, work your body line..." She staggered near the Buffet Pavilion, barely able to stand. Just then John saw her, grabbed her by the waist, and slipped her in line in front of him.

"Where were you?" asked Rosa, turning her head.

"The ladies room was packed," said Maria, barely audible.

"I looked there and couldn' find you."

"That's because I cut my hand and had to find a bandage," said Maria, showing her hand to her mother.

"Is it cut bad?"

"No, just a little tear. It'll be all right."

"I better look at it before it gets infected."

Rosa grabbed Maria's left hand and examined the cut. "Look! The stain on your palm is gone," she said.

"Yes, Mom. Everything's fine."

"Well, you gave your father and me some anxious moments. He's had these reservations for years and you missed the best part."

Maria saw Rosa's mouth moving, but barely heard what she said. The anger she felt toward her had melted away. In fact, she felt no anger toward anyone, and she didn't care what they said. She loved them.

The wrinkles on her parents' faces had smoothed over. Rosa seemed to be 40 pounds lighter and Sal wasn't coughing.

"Must be all the champagne," he said.

Rosa added, "I love this lighting. I look so much better in these old mirrors."

"You're both wonderful," Maria said.

The line snaked back around the 50th Street side of the building and re-entered the Rainbow Room. Then it broke and everyone applauded the band.

"Now tell me just how it happened," said Rosa, examining Maria's cut.

John came to her rescue, as the music of *If* filled the air. It was their song. He didn't have to ask Maria to dance; she reached out her arms and led John to the dance floor.

"I have some ideas for your paintings," she said.

"Later," he replied.

Maria tried to tell him something, but the words didn't come out. She was in John's arms.

John whispered, "For Auld Lang Synge?"
Maria laid her head on his shoulder.

> *If the world should stop revolving,*
> *Spinning slowly down to die.*
> *I'd spend the end with you,*
> *And when the world was through,*
> *Then one by one, the stars would all go out,*
> *And you and I would simply fly away.*